BITTER QUEEN

ADVANTAGE PLAY SERIES BOOK 4

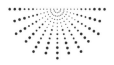

KELSIE RAE

Cover Art by Cover My Wagon Dragon Art

Editing by My Brother's Editor

Proofreading by Stephanie Taylor

November 2020 Edition

Published in the United States of America

BLURB

Diece is the right-hand man to the most powerful family in the Italian Mafia. He's ruthless, brutal, and has been tasked with protecting me after I stuck my neck out for his boss.

That doesn't mean I trust him, though.

Against my will, Diece whisks me away under the guise of keeping me safe, but I'm not about to exchange one prison for another.

When he finds out what I've been through at the hands of my previous captor, he begs me to let my guard down.

To let him in.

But if I do, he'll find out the truth, and I can't let that happen. Not just for me, but for his safety too.

He says he won't let anyone hurt me.

He has no idea who I'm running from.

PROLOGUE

DIECE

Her legs wobble as she follows me toward the shed. The brisk air is turning warmer as the sun peeks over the horizon in the distance, but even the blinding sun can't tear my gaze away from the sexy stranger.

Who the hell is this girl?

"I'm Diece, by the way," I introduce myself, breaking the uncomfortable silence. "I know Kingston mentioned me, but I figured I should probably introduce myself. And you're Queena?"

The only response I get is a piece of gravel being kicked across the sidewalk leading to the shed tucked behind Kingston Romano's massive house.

"Well, it's uh…it's nice to meet you." *I sound like a damn pussy.* "I don't know how long we're going to be together but—"

"We're not going to be together." Her voice is cold. Indifferent. And laced with disgust. Like I'm a piece of shit she stepped in, and she doesn't know how to clean it off.

My annoyance spikes, but I shove it aside. She's been held against her will for the past two weeks. Of course, she's going to be leery of strange men, especially when they've been tasked with keeping an eye on you for the foreseeable future.

"Sorry, Q," I apologize. "But you're stuck with me until Kingston tells me otherwise. You put a target on your back when you told a room full of very powerful men at Burlone's poker tournament that you work for the FBI."

She freezes when Burlone's name rolls off my tongue, but I don't blame her. He kidnapped her, tortured her, and planned to sell her as a sex slave before Kingston stepped in and framed Burlone for working with the FBI. But it was Q who stepped in and verified his bullshit accusation. I just wish she saw us as an ally instead of shoving the Romano family in the same box as Burlone Allegretti.

"Don't get me wrong. We're grateful," I continue, attempting to tread lightly. "There's a big possibility none of you would've made it out of there alive without your help. But it doesn't change the fact that you kind of screwed your-self over because of it. Kingston recognizes your sacrifice and is offering to protect you. You need to take him up on it."

"And if I don't want to?"

"Then you'll wind up in a ditch by the end of the week," I answer bluntly. She flinches at my brashness, causing a bolt of guilt to hit me straight in the chest. With a sigh, I try again. "Look, I know you've been dealt a shit hand, but now's your opportunity to make the most of it."

She peeks up at me through her thick upper lashes. "Are you asking me to trust you?"

I shrug. "Yeah. I guess I am."

"And what if I can't?"

"Listen, I don't know what happened—"

She starts marching toward the shed that holds Burlone and cuts me off. "I've trusted a lot of people in my life, and

2

every single one of them has let me down. What makes you any different?"

Her candor takes me aback, causing me to ask myself the same thing. I'm not a good guy. I've killed people. Crippled them. Sold drugs and weapons to people who definitely shouldn't be touching them.

The realization is harsh as I murmur, "I guess I don't know."

"Then I guess I can't trust you."

"Listen—"

"Where's the bat?" she asks as we reach the shed that holds Burlone. I'd promised she could use one against the bastard when we were in Kingston's office a few minutes ago. She's a feisty little thing. I'll give her that much. And bitter. So damn bitter that I'm surprised her pouty lips aren't pursed twenty-four-seven.

The shed door has a metal padlock hanging from the front, and I search my pockets for the keys Stefan handed off to me as we left the office.

"The bat's in here. Listen, if you want a chance to make Burlone hurt, then I'm going to need you to promise me something." Her eyes flash at the prospect of finally exacting her revenge against the guy who put her through Hell, and I know I have her full attention. "I need you to let me watch out for you until it's safe for you to leave."

"No deal," she grits out, looking around the expansive yard like a caged beast.

"Then I'm afraid I can't let you in here."

"Diece—"

My name on her lips makes my cock hard, but I ignore my physical response and try to focus on the conversation.

"I want to keep you safe, Q. But you need to let me."

Slowly, I watch as tears gather in her eyes before she hastily wipes them away. "How long?"

My brows furrow. "How long?"

"How long do I need to give you?"

"I don't know." I shrug. "Until it's safe for you to leave."

"So, I'm exchanging one prison for another?" Her voice cracks on the word *prison*, making my heart break right along with it.

"If that's how you have to look at it," I mutter, "Then, yes. But it's for your own good."

"And the only way you'll let me hurt Burlone is if I agree to it?"

I nod. "Yeah. That's the deal."

Squeezing her eyes shut tight, I watch a small part of her die inside before she whispers, "Open the door. I'll do whatever you want me to do, just…just let me hurt him."

I shove the key into the lock, then turn it and unlatch the shed. After, I flip the light switch on the wall to reveal a hunched body in the center of the empty room. Looks like Burlone hasn't woken up from the hit to his head. I smirk, knowing his skull is going to be pounding when he finally does.

"Come on in," I murmur to Queena.

Peering into the room, she releases a shaky breath before stepping over the threshold like she's afraid something is going to jump out and grab her.

There's a tall metal cabinet in the back corner, and I make my way over to it. Once it's opened, I wave my hand in front of the various tools designed to make someone hurt.

"Here ya go, Q. Go wild."

1

Q

M

y eyes nearly pop out of my head as I inspect my options. Knives of every shape and size. A hand-sized blow-torch I've seen used on the cooking channel to make crème brûlée. Pliers. A hammer. Chisels. Cigar cutters. I catch myself hyperventilating as I continue my perusal in a daze when Diece gently touches the small of my back. I nearly jump out of my skin. Twisting away from him, he raises his hands into the air before offering an apology.

"Shit, Queena. I didn't mean to scare you. Are you okay?"

I nod, though I can feel the lie from the top of my head to the tips of my toes.

No. I'm not okay.

"The baseball bat's over here, but you're welcome to whatever you want. Just make sure you leave something for Ace. She has her own beef with Burlone too." He points to the lower half of the cabinet, where a couple of baseball bats sit as the memory of my conversation with Ace flutters through my mind.

Again, I nod because I'm not sure I could talk right now, even if I tried.

Yeah.

She does have her own beef with him. And she's being generous letting me have the first swing. If it were Sei strapped into that chair, there's no way I'd let her go first. There's no way I'd let *anyone* touch him except me.

Hands shaking, I reach for the wooden bat. My knuckles are white with how hard I grip the handle, but my palms are sweaty, and I don't want to risk dropping it. I can't let Diece see how weak I feel.

How weak I *am* after everything I've been through.

"What now?" I whisper, peeking up at him.

"Now, you wake him up."

"And how would I do that?"

He smirks. "Well, you can do it nicely and build the anticipation before the first hit, or you can do it the hard way with a single swing to the knee."

Considering my options, I murmur, "I want him to know it's coming."

"Good choice."

Digging through the cabinet, he grabs a little canister and offers it to me.

Hesitantly, I take it, making sure not to touch his calloused hands.

"What's this?" I ask.

"Smelling salts. It's ammonia. Just put it under his nose, and he'll wake up in no time."

"You mean that actually works?" My tone is laced with disbelief.

He grins. It's so boyish and carefree, you'd think we were discussing a sitcom or comedy act.

"Like a charm," he answers.

Shaking off the effects of his smile, I do as I'm told and twist off the lid on the canister, then walk over to an unconscious Burlone. As I put the small canister under his nose, a bit of the salt spills onto Burlone's stained dress shirt. I'm shaking. With every ounce of effort and determination I can find, I shove aside my fear, along with the knowledge that I'll never be comfortable around a man again. Even the one watching me near the sociopath toy box.

Within seconds, Burlone wakes up with a gasp.

"What the fuck?" he murmurs, disoriented. Blinking rapidly, a very confused Burlone looks around the room. "Where the hell am I?"

Frozen, I simply stare at the bastard who ruined me, unsure of what to do next.

"Hello, Burlone," Diece says conversationally, stepping in to back me up. "Q here would like to show you her appreciation for your hospitality over the past two weeks."

Squinting his eyes, Burlone looks me up and down before tugging against the zip ties around his wrists that keep him strapped to the metal chair. "You! This is all your fault! She's part of the FBI, Diece. Don't listen to a word she has to say. She's a liar. A filthy slut—"

I cut him off by slapping him as hard as I can. The palm of my hand stings from the impact, but the satisfaction I feel as his head snaps to one side and the angry mark on his cheek is enough to soothe it.

"Shut up, Burlone," I spit. "I don't want to hear a single word come out of your mouth unless I ask you a question. Understand?"

"Who the hell do you think you are, you filthy—"

Smack. My palm tingles, slightly burning as I hit him again.

"I said, shut up," I seethe. "Do you remember what you

said to me when we first met? How you were going to sell me to someone who would make me scream? How you wished it could be you, but you needed the money, and my virginity would go for a pretty penny?" The words nearly get clogged in my throat, but I choke them out. "Well, now it's my turn."

Lifting the bat, I aim for his leg like Diece instructed and savor the sound of his knee cap being crushed, accompanied by his crying as soon as the wood connects with it. The combination is like a balm to my soul, finally easing the ache inside of me.

So I do it again.

And again.

Until Diece's thick forearms wrap around my waist, and he tugs me away, bringing me back to the present instead of the memories that I've been drowning in.

"Enough, Q. Enough."

Looking over at Burlone, I finally see the damage I've done. His face is a messy pulp of skin and blood. His head hangs limp on his shoulders as his shirt soaks up the crimson liquid that flows onto it. It's horrific and would've given me nightmares before I was kidnapped. But now I'm too jaded to care. His chest rises and falls unevenly, proving he's still alive while I'm left feeling dead on the inside.

Angry, I lift the bat again, but Diece grabs it from me. "It's enough," he repeats.

I shake my head back and forth as my fraying emotions finally get the best of me.

"It'll never be enough," I sob. Clinging to Diece, I finally give in and grieve the loss of the girl I once was compared to the stranger I've become. "Never."

"Shh," he whispers, squeezing me a little harder in his embrace. "You made him hurt. And now, Ace will get her turn. Then King."

"But why don't I feel better?" I choke out.

"Because his pain didn't lessen yours. And it never will."

The truth is gut-wrenching, and I collapse into Diece's arms before begging him to take me away. I just…I can't stand the scent of Burlone's blood any longer.

Who have I become?

Q

Diece carries me to a sleek, black car before slipping me into the passenger seat. When I don't move a muscle, my new prison guard carefully buckles the seatbelt over my lap as if I'm a toddler. Then he gets behind the wheel and backs out of the driveway.

My breathing is shallow as I chew on my thumbnail and stare out the side window. The trees blur together before they're replaced with graffitied buildings, then transform into rolling pastures speckled with livestock.

Where are you taking me?

The question rests on the tip of my tongue, but I don't bother to voice it aloud. It wouldn't do me any good, anyway.

I don't know how much time passes before Diece finally breaks the silence. "Where are you from?"

I stay silent.

"Have you ever been to the country before?"

My eyes glaze as I continue to stare out the window.

"Do you like animals?" he tries again. "Matteo has a stable at his estate. He used to have horses and shit, but I'm not sure if he still does."

Blinking back tears, I dig my teeth into the pad of my thumb until I'm positive the skin will break.

With a sigh, he turns down a long, winding road off the highway. The nearest town is at least thirty minutes away. If he wants to kill me, or rape me, or hurt me, this is the opportunity for it.

"We're here," he mutters when the car rounds the corner.

My heart drops to my stomach as my new prison comes into view. The place is huge, with a gray stone exterior and lush green vines weaving up the sides. A set of steps leads to a heavy oak door that looks like it could've belonged to a castle from the fifteenth century.

Hell, it could've belonged to the beast himself in *Beauty and the Beast*.

But this isn't a fairy-tale. It's a nightmare.

And no matter how hard I've tried, I can't wake up.

With a twist of the key, Diece turns the car off. Then we sit in silence. Again. I can feel his stare, but I don't bother to look at him as he waits a few seconds before announcing, "Let's get settled, shall we?"

I don't move.

"Come on, Q. I'll show you inside."

Unfolding himself from inside the tiny car, he closes the door then waits for me to follow him. When I don't, his jaw tightens.

"You promised me, Q," he calls before turning around and holding my stare through the windshield. "You promised you'd do whatever I asked if I let you hurt Burlone. I kept my end of the deal. Now, I need you to keep yours. Will you please get out of the car and come inside?"

Please.

It's funny. That word never worked for me when I was begging Sei to stop. When I was pleading for him not to hurt me. Not to use me. Not to make me do all the despicable things he made me do.

The squeak of the hinges on the passenger door makes me jump as Diece tugs it open then offers his hand for me to take.

"Please?" he repeats.

Squeezing my eyes shut, I fight off the urge to run. Then I slip out of the car without his help. The gravel crunches beneath his shoes as he steps back to give me plenty of space. With a glare, I cross my arms and wait for his next command.

Because they *always* demand more.

3

DIECE

"Ladies first," I mutter, motioning to the entrance of Matteo's place.

With her chin to her chest and her eyes on the ground, she heads to the entrance. I follow behind her, then use the large gold knocker to announce our presence.

Matteo Moretti answers a few seconds later. The bastard stepped back from the family business when his father started strengthening their family's connection with Burlone Allegretti. But he's proven to be a friend of the Romanos when we've had our backs against the wall. And today is no different. His gaze lazily scans us both up and down before he steps back to allow us to enter his family's summer house. The one that's been vacant for years and belongs to one of Burlone's associates. It's the last place anyone would look for us. Especially Q's enemies.

"Come on in," he offers.

"Thanks."

As we step inside, he replies, "Don't mention it. Lou told me to pick up a few things before you got here. They're in the west wing."

Queena's mouth twitches, hinting at her beauty, but she keeps her eyes on her hands and continues to wring them like a dirty dishrag.

"Something funny?" I ask in a low voice that's only meant for her.

With a subtle shake of her head, she keeps her lips shut.

Shocker.

I sigh. "Q, this is Matteo. He's...a friend of the family. Matteo, this is Q."

"Nice to meet you," Matteo replies, though I can almost see the wheels turning in his head as he scans her up and down another time. I don't know what Kingston said to convince him to help us. And I have no idea if he knows that Q helped bring Kingston's plan to fruition during the poker tournament at Burlone's estate. The plan that led to Matteo's uncle's arrest less than forty-eight hours ago.

It's not like they were on good terms, but he's still a Moretti.

I do know one thing, though. He's not an idiot, and if Kingston trusts him, then so do I.

Matteo might insist that he keeps his hands clean, but the bastard knows everything and everyone in this business. He might even know Q's true identity.

But I sure as hell don't.

After another moment of silence, Matteo decides, "Let me show you to your rooms." Turning on his heel, he leads us up a set of dark, wooden stairs to the second floor that splits into two sections, one to my left and one to my right. There are two long, winding hallways at the top. Both appear to be lined with doors on each side as he guides us down to the left section of rooms. When we reach the end of it, Matteo pushes open the last door.

"Here we are. There's a bathroom and a walk-in closet through that door." He points to the door hidden at the back of the bedroom. "I used to have my groceries delivered, along with take-out, when I didn't feel like cooking. The number is on the kitchen table on the main floor. Any questions?"

Q remains quiet and doesn't even bother to look around. Annoyed by her lack of gratitude, and desperate for a minute to breathe outside of her presence, I rock back on my heels and answer, "I think we're good. Q, why don't you take a shower or something. I'll be back in a few."

Matteo and I exit the room, then I close the door behind me, but a panicked Queena wrenches it open almost instantly. Her chest is heaving, and her eyes are open wide in fear as she begs, "Please let me keep it open. I promise I won't go anywhere, and I'll do what you tell me. I just...I can't...." She doesn't finish her sentence but lets her voice trail off as she continues to hyperventilate right before my eyes.

I think it's because there are far too many ways that she could finish that statement. She can't function. She can't deal with the shit she's been through. She can't trust anyone, let alone the guy who's trying to protect her. She can't do a lot of shit.

But instead of pointing out the obvious, I raise my hands in surrender and take a cautious step back to give her some space.

"Sure thing. It's your room." Then I follow Matteo to his security room on the opposite side of the house. I can feel her watching me before I round the corner, but I don't bother to turn around and call her out for it. Besides, it's not a crime to be curious. Hell, it proves she's still alive. And sometimes, I think she needs a reminder.

As soon as I enter the security room, Matteo crosses his arms and gets right to the point. "So...who is she?"

"She's none of your concern."

With a dry laugh, he shakes his head. "Sure, she isn't. She

15

wouldn't have anything to do with my uncle's incarceration, would she?"

I stay quiet, though I'm sure he can see the slight tic in my jaw. For someone trying to distance himself from family business, the bastard knows far too much.

Matteo smiles before changing the subject. "Lou didn't mention how long you'd both be staying…."

"That's because we don't have a firm answer yet."

"Well, I guess we'll start with a few weeks then. You have my number. I also left the maid's number and the grocery delivery service contact info in the kitchen."

"Yeah, on the table. You mentioned that."

"You're lucky you're not kicking me out of my house," he quips, ignoring my asinine remark.

"Sorry for the short notice. But thank you for your help," I add.

"I owed King. Now, we're even."

"Good to know. Do I need to know about anything in here?" Motioning to the room, I take in the monitors, keyboard, and desktop that looks like a regular office on steroids.

He waves me off. "Nah. It's just your usual shit. Since this place is out in the middle of nowhere, the security cameras usually only go off when a cow is on our grounds, but I'll hook up your phone to get notifications."

"Thanks."

"Sure thing," he returns.

"How could you tell it was her?" I demand, unable to help myself.

Plopping down into an office chair, he confides, "She was the first face on Uncle Moretti's email, and the only one he cared to see. He'd planned on purchasing her, but Burlone said he already had a buyer lined up. Good ol' Uncle Moretti was sorely disappointed, as I'm sure you can imagine."

"He's not used to being told no."

"No, he's not. He planned on reaching out to a guy named...Johnson? He was going to offer him more money to keep her, but that obviously didn't work out since he's a little busy in prison. And he's under the impression Kingston took care of her."

Rolling my shoulders, I mutter, "Yeah...about that...."

"I don't give a shit about good ol' Uncle Moretti." Matteo laughs, amused by my half-assed attempt to apologize before sobering with his next words. "And she doesn't look like a Fed to me. But she's too stunning for her own good, D. I suggest you figure out how the hell to alter her appearance. Quickly. Word travels fast, and it's only a matter of time before they come looking for her––the girl who got away."

"What else have you heard?" I prod.

"That she isn't who she appears to be."

I cock my head to the side. "Do you know who she is?"

Pulling up a live feed of the hallway that leads to her bedroom, he studies it carefully. The door is wide open, but there isn't any movement.

"Answer the question," I demand.

With his gaze glued to the screen, he concludes, "She's just a broken girl who doesn't know how to put herself back together again." Clearing his throat, he tears his attention away from the video feed and looks up at me. "Be gentle with her."

"I won't hurt her."

"I meant emotionally," he clarifies.

"I'll keep that in mind."

He nods. "Good. I left all the items Lou mentioned on your bed in the room across from hers. I don't know if hair dye will be enough to hide her identity, but it's worth a shot. And like I said, let me know if you need anything else.

There's a keypad on the door to this room. The code is 0-0-1-0-0."

"Why so simple?"

"Because everyone expects a guy like me to have something complicated. I figured I'd just give them the bird and tell them to fuck off instead."

I laugh as recognition dawns on me. The code signifies his knuckles. While the majority of numbers are low, the middle digit is high in the air. As if he's literally giving them the bird. "Clever," I compliment. "And thanks again, Matteo. Have you heard any unrest from the other families?"

"It's a little early to tell. Lucca Russo is being a bit of a bitch about the transition, but he's harmless. If you found someone in your ranks to marry his sister, Emilia, he'd probably shut right up. He just wants to keep his family's status without having to lift a finger. I heard his father had been setting up a betrothal with one of Burlone's soldiers, but it fell through when all hell broke loose less than forty-eight hours ago."

I smirk. "That won't be a problem. Stefan has wanted her for years. What about everyone else?"

He shrugs and leans back in his office chair. "Nothing too out of the ordinary. Now they're just fighting with each other like a pack of wolves over a scrap of meat. Who'll be crowned the next king of the underworld when their fearless leaders were all whisked away in handcuffs?"

"Dex," I answer him.

Brow quirked, he repeats, "Dex?"

"He was being groomed for the position, anyway. Why not give them what they want?"

"And if they don't back Dex?"

"Then they go in the ground. We're going to extract anyone who wants to continue selling *fruit* to the highest bidder."

Fruit.

What a twisted way to talk about human beings. Like they're nothing but an object.

Matteo kicks his feet up onto the desk then laces his fingers behind his head as if he has all the time in the world. But it doesn't hide his flash of surprise as he clarifies, "You plan on eradicating the entire human trafficking industry?"

"In this part of the country, yeah. We've seen what it does to women. *Our* women," I clarify. "Regina. Ace."

"And Q?" he challenges.

I hesitate. "Yeah. And Q."

"Interesting," he notes.

That same tic in my jaw returns with a vengeance as I grit out, "Kingston promised to protect her."

"So, it has nothing to do with the way you look at her?" He scoffs. "Keep telling yourself that. But what makes you think the Romano family can pull it off? You've never been in the skin trade."

"King's dad didn't want to make things messy for the family by sticking his nose where it didn't belong. But Burlone crossed that line and left us no choice as soon as he tried to frame us by doing business on our docks."

He scratches his jaw before resting his elbows on his knees. "I remember hearing about that. Obviously, thinking he could use Kingston was Burlone's biggest mistake. But I think you're smart to take control while everyone is left scrambling."

"Me too. Kingston might be young, but he knows his shit."

"Yeah, he seems to be fitting in as *Boss* quite nicely." An amused Matteo studies me closely before muttering, "I'm just glad I'm on your side."

I lift my chin in agreement. "Thanks again for letting us stay."

"No problem. I'm heading out in a few."

"Sounds good."

Twisting the door handle, I head back down the hall toward our bedrooms. Q's door is still wide open, but she hasn't moved a muscle from where we left her ten minutes ago.

A sigh escapes me before I lean against the doorjamb and mutter, "Hey."

She doesn't acknowledge me.

"Do you want to shower or anything? Maybe get some sleep?"

And maybe not stare at the wall like a crazy person?

More silence.

Rubbing my hand over my face, I stalk closer to make sure I'm in her line of sight. "Q, I'm gonna need you to start talking to me."

"I thought men liked their women silent." There's an edge in her voice that gives me hope she isn't completely dead inside.

"Not *this* silent," I joke before taking in her bruised complexion. The makeup that'd been caked on her face since the tournament has slowly rubbed away to reveal black and blue undertones that would make a UFC fighter cringe. "How's your face feeling?"

Confused, she drops her gaze down to the ground but doesn't say anything.

"Answer me," I press, keeping my tone soft as if she's a scared little creature.

Peeking up at me through her thick, dark upper lashes, she mumbles, "I-I don't know what's wrong with my face."

"Have you looked in the mirror?"

Again. Silence.

I fight the urge to shake her and squeeze my hands into tight fists at my sides. "Answer me, Q."

"I haven't looked in the mirror since the night I was taken."

My eyes widen before I cover my shock with indifference. What the hell did they do to her?

"You should probably take a look at the damage," I return. "Matteo said the bathroom is over here."

Making sure not to touch her, I guide her into the white marble master bathroom, then stop her in front of the mirror. Q's attention is firmly on her feet, but her slender frame is quaking like a leaf. So bad that I'm afraid she might collapse onto the floor.

What. The. Hell.

"Hey," I whisper. My palms itch to touch her, but I restrain myself. "What's wrong?"

She shakes her head and squeezes her eyes shut. "I can't look."

"Why?"

Her lips turn white from the pressure of her teeth digging into them before a shallow breath slips past her lips. "Because it won't be me in the mirror."

"What do you mean?"

"It's not me," she repeats. Her voice cracks before she sniffs softly. "I'm gone. And now, I'm terrified to see the girl looking back at me in my own reflection because she'll be a stranger. And I can't bear the thought of it. I can't look at my long blonde hair without hearing his—" Her mouth snaps shut before her eyes widen in fear, and she looks over at me.

"Tell me," I demand.

She shakes her head.

"Tell me," I repeat with a bit more force.

Lower lip quivering, she whispers, "He loved my hair." The blood drains from her face. "Loved how it was naturally blonde. Loved how long it was so that he could wrap it around his fist. Loved to pull on it until clumps would come out in his hand. Loved to drag me around the room with it if I ever disobeyed him. Loved to pet it when I'd been a good girl and did whatever he asked of me. He loved it." She swallows before a bitterness overcomes her. One that's so strong, I can almost taste it. Then her hatred-filled gaze meets mine, and she spits, "And now, I *hate* it."

Shit.

"Wait right here," I order.

I stride to my room and dig through the sacks on my bed that Matteo had mentioned. When I find a pair of scissors and a couple of boxes of hair dye, I return to her bathroom and carefully set them on the counter in front of her.

"Do you want to say goodbye to the girl you used to be before we get rid of her?" I ask.

She shakes her head. "No. I said goodbye to her the moment he touched me for the first time."

My mouth floods with bile, but I swallow it back and slide off my Armani jacket, leaving me in a white button-up shirt that's still stained with Burlone's blood. Rolling up the sleeves, I grab the boxes of hair dye and start reading the directions on the back of them.

"What are you doing?" she whispers, cautiously watching me from the corner of her eye.

"Which one do you prefer?"

There are two options––a soft, silver blue, and a dark, almost black, navy color. I raise them for her to inspect, but she doesn't bother to look at either of them.

"Whatever you want," she replies in a monotone voice. The same glaze I'm growing accustomed to covers her eyes as she stares blankly at me.

"You're allowed to make your own decisions, Q."

She scoffs. "Bullshit."

"I'm serious. Don't think about what the old Q would want. Don't think about what the girl in Burlone's captivity would want. Think about the girl in front of me right now. What does she want?"

Squeezing her eyes closed, a single tear slips down her cheek. "She wants to disappear."

The air whooshes out of my lungs as though I've been sucker-punched. This wasn't part of the job description. How the hell am I supposed to fix this girl when she doesn't want to be fixed?

Wrenching open the box in my left hand without giving a shit which color it is, I start mixing the ingredients together then section her hair the way the directions explain. We don't say a word as I paint the blonde strands with blue ink while ignoring the patches of scabs that cling to her scalp.

Once I'm finished, I wash my hands, then pull out my cell from the front pocket of my slacks and set the timer.

Then we wait. In silence. Because I don't feel like asking any more questions that are going to reveal what really happened to an innocent girl at the hands of a sick mother-fucker who died earlier this morning.

Call me a coward, but I can't take it anymore. Not right now.

And it's not like she's one for small talk, anyway.

Sliding to the ground, I press my back against the white wall and look up at a comatose Q who hasn't moved a muscle since I brought her in here. She reminds me of a puppet, waiting for someone to pull the strings and tell her what to do as if she can't make her own decisions or think for herself.

She really is broken. And I don't know if I'm the right man for the job to put her back together again.

Hell, I don't even know if it's possible.

Even though it kills me inside, I motion to the tile floor and mutter, "You can sit down if you want."

Like a good little puppet, she crosses her legs and sits

down but leaves a solid two-foot radius of empty space around her while staring blankly at the wall across from us.

She'll never trust me.

With my elbows on my bent knees, I tear my gaze away from her and watch the minutes tick by.

The timer dings a little while later. Pushing myself up from the tile ground, I offer my hand to help her do the same. Q stares at it for a few seconds like it's a cobra about to strike. She releases a shaky breath. Then she takes it. Her hand is tiny as mine swallows hers whole, reminding me how fragile she really is. Once she's on her feet, I release my hold and squeeze the back of my neck.

"We're, uh, we're supposed to wash your hair now. Do you want to just take a shower, or do you need my help?"

Her lower lip quivers as a soft breath escapes her. I'm not sure what I've said, but I backpedal, "I can help if you need it. I just figured you might want some privacy. I know it's been a long day."

Her silence suffocates me before she peeks up at me and admits, "I'm not sure I know what privacy is anymore."

"Then I think you need it even more. Do you prefer showers or baths?"

She drops her gaze back to the ground, but she doesn't answer me.

The clear glass shower door is heavy as I pull it open and turn on the hot water. When my attention catches on a razor, I freeze, then take it out of the small space while hating the fact that suicide even crossed my mind.

"I'll just be outside," I announce.

Her dainty fingers reach for my forearm and showcase the contrast between her pale skin and my olive tone as she prevents me from leaving. Curious, I drag my stare from her innocent touch and up to her bruised face. Her chin drops down to her chest before she releases her hold, pushes her long, painted hair over one shoulder, then gives me her back.

"W-will you unzip me?"

Without a word, I take the tiny piece of metal that holds her stained dress together between my fingertips. The zipper slowly reveals inch after inch of soft, milky white skin marred with fresh cuts and purple bruises. Turning my head away from the evidence of her abuse, I finish tugging the zipper down before it stops at the base of her spine.

The fabric drops to the floor and pools around our feet. Then a very naked Q glances over her shoulder at me with big, doe eyes. Tempting me. Testing me. Daring me to be the man she thinks I am.

But I'm not him.

And I hate that she can't see that.

Clearing my throat, I turn away and grab the scissors off the counter. "I'll be in your room. There should be shampoo and shit in the shower. I'll go find something for you to change into when you're finished." Forcing myself to look back at her, I keep my expression indifferent and ask, "Do you want the door open or closed?"

"Open," she whispers, holding my stare. The air is electric, threatening to consume me if her eyes weren't filled with so much hatred.

But they are. And it's that bitterness that convinces me to leave.

With a nod, I hold the scissors and razor in one hand, then push the door as far open as it will go before getting the hell out of there.

4

Q

The hot water burns my back as I rinse the dye from my long hair. It's almost a blue-gray color with a hint of purple. Mesmerized, I watch it swirl down the drain. A ghost of a smile spreads across my face before disappearing just as quickly.

I actually kind of like it.

As the water runs clear, I glance toward the door that leads to the bedroom, expecting to find Diece watching me. But his shadowed figure is absent. Sliding onto my butt, I let the water wash over me in scalding rivulets while the last thirty minutes play out on repeat.

He didn't touch me.

Even as I stood less than six inches away from him––*naked*––he didn't take advantage. He didn't even *look*. What does that mean?

It was almost easier in Sei's captivity because I knew exactly what to expect from everyone around me. But here? I'm left confused and on edge. I don't know what to do. I don't know what to think. I don't know what to believe.

Why didn't he touch me?

The water starts to cool, making goosebumps spread along my bare skin, so I push myself up and grab the dark, fluffy towel hanging on the rod outside of the glass shower. I flinch as it brushes against my sensitive flesh, then wrap it around my chest, tucking one corner between my breasts before crossing my arms and venturing into the bedroom.

A folded, extra-large T-shirt and sleep shorts sit on the edge of the bed, but my captor is nowhere to be seen. Convinced he's hiding somewhere so he can sneak a peek of my bare body, I squat down to pick up the clothes then hide away in the bathroom to get dressed. I still can't manage to close the damn door, though. Anytime I try, the walls come barreling in until I can't breathe. Claustrophobia is a bitch.

The T-shirt is a faded black, but it's soft. Comfortable. The worn material acts like a soothing blanket as it slides against my freshly cleaned skin, and it doesn't show my nipples through the dark color. Satisfied, I slip on the shorts before realizing they're men's boxers. My expression sours when a soft knock at the door grabs my attention.

"Hey," D interrupts, but he keeps his gaze glued to the floor as he hovers near the entrance from the hallway. "Are you decent?"

I want to laugh but restrain myself as I look over at him. Dark, wavy hair. Strong jaw. And muscle after freaking muscle. The guy's huge. And terrifying. Even though he's shown me nothing but kindness, I just...can't trust him. I know what those muscles can do. What those fists can do.

My lips pull into a thin line, refusing to answer him.

It's another test, though I doubt he knows it.

Brows pinched, I wait for him to sneak a peek, but his eyes stay glued to the floor as I stay hidden in the back corner of the bathroom.

"Q?" he calls gruffly after another few seconds. "Can I come in? Or do you need another minute?"

Swallowing thickly, I give in and choke out, "Yeah. I'm decent."

He lifts his gaze, steps into the bedroom, then searches the empty bathroom for a split second before his eyes land on me. My breath hitches as he scans me from head to toe. But it isn't sexual. It's as if he's checking off boxes in his head to make sure I'm taken care of. But why? I don't know how I feel about it––the fact that he acts like he cares.

"Sorry about the clothes," he grunts as he finishes his inspection. "Matteo forgot to pick something up for you other than the hair dye, so you're stuck with my stuff for now. I'm not comfortable with us going out, so I'm going to have someone drop some shit off. You ready to finish your makeover?"

My mouth twitches with another smile as the word makeover slips out of his mouth.

"Something funny?" he challenges, showcasing his amusement.

I shake my head.

Wagging the pair of scissors from earlier back and forth, he drops the subject and asks, "Do you want to do the honors, or do you want me to?"

Oh. Right.

My shoulders hunch, but I don't answer him. It's not like I actually have a choice in the matter, and I've been avoiding the mirror like the plague anyway.

"Q." He exhales. I've pissed him off. Bracing myself for a fist, he surprises me by setting the scissors on the counter and lacing his fingers behind his head until his biceps are bulging. "I can't imagine the shit you've been through, but you're allowed to communicate with me. If you don't want to cut it, we don't have to. The color has already changed your appearance more than I expected. We'll do whatever––"

"Cut it."

He arches his brow. "You want me to do it?"

I nod while continuing to ignore my reflection in the mirror. I can't look.

"You sure?"

"Yes," I whisper.

"Do you care how short we do it?"

It's almost down to my butt right now and has been for as long as I can remember. The idea of cutting it off is surreal.

"Q?"

"Whatever you want," I tell him.

"This isn't about me or what I want, Q. This is about you."

A scoff slips out of me before I can stop it as I point out, "Nothing is about me."

"This is," he argues. "It's your hair. You get to decide how short we go."

"Fine." Licking my lips, I cross my arms and answer, "Short."

He studies me for a few seconds before deciding that's the only answer he's going to get. Stepping forward, my captor pushes all of my hair behind my shoulders until it hangs limply down my back.

Then he starts cutting. And with every snip of the scissors, a weight feels like it's being lifted from my shoulders. The cool air kisses the back of my neck by the time he's finished while the discarded hair tickles my bare feet as it lies on the marble tile around me.

A few minutes later, his gruff voice breaks the silence. "Finished." With a satisfied nod, he examines his handy work then announces, "Damn, I'm good. Take a look."

I close my eyes and suck in a deep breath, making sure to fill my lungs to full capacity before letting it all out in a slow exhale as I search for the courage to face the new me. The one who's broken. The one who's lost. The one who's afraid of her own shadow and is terrified of her past. Her present. And her future.

I can't do this.

"Q?" Diece prods with a gentle voice.

Unable to ignore it any longer, I open my eyes, turn to the mirror, and gasp. I don't know who the girl in the mirror is, but her face is mottled with black and blue, and her hair is… well, it's kind of badass and reaches just below her chin. Carefully, I run my fingers along my swollen cheekbone as I inspect the damage from Sei's fists while almost forgetting that I have an audience.

"Does it hurt?" Diece breathes beside me.

A breath of laughter slips out of me, but there isn't any humor in it. "It *always* hurts. I remember thinking I'd get numb to it all, but…." My voice trails off as I blink back tears.

"Tell me."

"I felt *everything* every single time. I *still* feel everything," I correct myself, though my tone is indifferent.

His hands tighten into fists at his sides as he watches me carefully. I can tell he wants to comfort me but doesn't know how. He's not the only one who's helpless, though.

I wish I knew how to make the pain go away too.

"He's gone now," Diece reminds me, rocking back on his heels. "Burlone can't hurt you anymore."

What?

"Burlone didn't hurt me," I tell him.

Confused, he asks, "Then who hurt you, Q?"

My mouth floods with bile, but I swallow it back.

"Tell me," he pleads.

"Sei did."

5

DIECE

A high-pitched scream breaks the silence in the dark house, rousing me from a deep sleep. It scatters the haze of exhaustion that usually clings to me at three in the morning, pushing me to jump into action. I reach for my gun that rests on the nightstand, then rush across the hall to obliterate the source of Q's pain.

Her room is painted in black as she tosses and turns in her bed. But she's alone.

I drop my gun-wielding arm to my side and turn back to my room when another bloodcurdling scream ricochets off the walls. Facing her again, I rub my eyes and push aside my panic.

What the hell am I supposed to do?

Her back arches off the mattress as her legs tangle in the sheets that act like angry hands, clawing at her limbs to keep her in place. But I'm helpless to save her from the demons haunting her dreams. They aren't real. And she probably wouldn't want my help anyway. Squeezing the back of my neck, I watch her from the shadows as she pulls her knees to her chest and curls into a tiny ball on her side before she whimpers, "Please, stop. No, no, please—"

My legs eat up the distance between myself and the bed before I sit on the edge and shake her gently. "Q. Q, wake up. Wake up. It's alright."

She squirms against me, wiggling out of my grasp when another sob escapes her. "No! Please—"

"Q." I shake her harder, desperate to make the monsters disappear. "Q, wake up."

"Stop! Stop!" she shrieks.

"Q!" Yanking her up, I bring her to my bare chest and wrap my arms around her, then rock her back and forth. "Q, wake up."

Her trimmed nails dig into my bare back as she finally wakes up and cries, "He's here! He's here!"

"Shh," I murmur, rubbing my hand along the cotton T-shirt plastered to her sweaty frame. "He's not here, Q. He's gone. I promise."

"He was here—"

"It was a dream. Just a dream."

Registering my words, a silence envelops the room as she attempts to steady her staggered breathing. But she doesn't pull away. She burrows closer to my chest and releases a shaky exhale before replacing it with an even shakier inhale.

"Shhh," I whisper. "It's okay."

"W-where is he?" Her voice is hoarse and is laced with a desperation that guts me.

"He was arrested. He's in the FBI's custody."

Her tears drench my chest as she pulls away and looks up at me.

"You're sure?"

"Yeah. Dex took care of it."

"How? I need details, Diece," she pleads.

Recalling the conversation before I left, I tell her, "Dex

said he tied Sei up and threw him in one of Burlone's closets where the tournament was held. They took him in with the rest of the bastards who buy and sell women. He's gone, Q. Promise."

"He's in prison?" she asks.

"Yeah. That's what I've been told."

"And you're positive? He doesn't know where I am? Wouldn't be able to find me? No matter what?"

"Yeah. Positive."

Her voice reaches a higher pitch as she demands, "And what about anyone else? Could anyone else find me if they were looking?"

"What? Who?"

"Just answer the question," she spits.

"No. The only people who know your whereabouts are Kingston, Matteo, you, and me," I tell her. "You're safe here, Q. I promise. I won't let anyone hurt you."

A spark ignites inside of her at my words, causing her to blaze with a fury that's so deep and angry, I'm surprised I don't combust on the spot.

She scoots back a few more feet before giving me a seething glare that's filled with contempt. "Why?"

"What?"

"Why won't you let anyone hurt me?" she demands.

"Excuse me?"

"Answer the question."

"You want me to tell you why I refuse to let anyone hurt you?" I can't help the sarcasm that slips into my question. She's lost her damn mind.

"Yeah. That's what I want you to tell me."

"Because I'm a decent human being?" I offer, my voice dripping with the same sarcasm as before while I race to catch up with why the hell she's suddenly pissed at me.

Hello, Dr. Jekyll and Mr. Hyde.

Surprising me with her malice, she scoffs. "Says the big, bad mafia man. Tell me, Diece, how many damsels have you saved, huh? Did they suck you off to say thank you? Is that what you want from me? Or maybe it's my precious virginity that you're hoping to take. Is that it? I got big news for you, buddy. All my other holes have already been used over and over again, so I'm afraid you'll be disappointed. My hymen might be intact, but my innocence has already been ripped away from me in ways you can't even imagine. Now, get out of my room and keep your empty promises to yourself."

Feeling whiplashed, I jerk away from her. "Q—"

"I said get out!" she shouts, shoving me away from her. I stand to my full height and rub my hand against my face as I find myself helpless for the first time in my life.

"What do you want me to say, Q?"

Pulling a pillow to her chest, she curls onto her side and stares blankly at the wall behind me. But she doesn't answer me.

It's like I don't exist anymore.

Not to her.

The realization burns, though I refuse to acknowledge why.

And it's all because I promised to keep her safe. Maybe she's right, though. Maybe she doesn't need a hero. Maybe she needs to learn how to defend herself. And I'm going to teach her how.

I SLEEP LIKE SHIT, TOSSING AND TURNING ALL NIGHT, BUT I'M grateful when I don't wake up to any more screaming from Q's room. In the kitchen, I find some eggs and whip together a quick breakfast before knocking on Q's door with a plate in hand.

She doesn't acknowledge my presence even though I can see her sitting on her bed.

Fighting back my annoyance, I call out, "Hey, can I come in?"

Silence.

"Q, can I come in? Please? I brought breakfast."

More silence.

"It's bacon and eggs. Nice and fresh."

When she doesn't bother to look at me, I curse under my breath and take a step back toward the stairs before a soft squeak from her room makes me pause. Unfolding herself from the bed, she pads over to me while I try to ignore how sexy she looks in my T-shirt and boxers. Her ashy blue hair is a mess as she tucks it behind her ear, but she doesn't say a word when she reaches me.

"Can I come in?" I ask gently.

Lips pursed, she gives in and waves her arm in front of her like it's a silent welcome banner that says, *come right in.*

My annoyance sparks into amusement as I witness her display.

Damn, she's cute.

Stepping inside, I set the plate of hot food on the nightstand. Her eyes dart over to it, and I can almost see her mouth watering, but she doesn't reach for it or take a bite.

"You can eat it," I tell her.

"I'm not hungry."

"Bullshit. I brought food up to your room last night after we cut your hair, and you didn't touch it. It's been at least twenty-four hours, Q. Why won't you eat it?"

Her teeth dig into her lower lip, but she doesn't answer me, making my earlier amusement disappear.

"Do you think I drugged it or something?"

With a one-shouldered shrug, she climbs back onto the

bed, then grabs the same pillow from last night and tucks it against her chest.

Taking the fork on her plate, I shove a massive bite of eggs into my mouth, then steal a slice of bacon and toss it in there too. She watches me chew but doesn't move until I swallow and offer her the fork.

She stares at it for a few seconds before finding the courage to take it from me. Hands shaking, she scoops up a small piece of scrambled egg. With her eyes on mine, her lips wrap around the utensil before she chews and swallows.

Then her manners evaporate, and she devours the entire meal, moaning as soon as the salty bacon touches her tongue. My chuckle mingles with her soft groan of appreciation as I sit down in an armchair tucked in the corner of her room.

With a contented sigh, she sets the fork down, then rests against the headboard and looks over at me with those same doe eyes that could bring a man to his knees.

"Thank you," she whispers.

"You're welcome," I return before leaning forward to rest my elbows on my knees. "Can I ask you something?"

After another minute of studying me, she gives me a jerky nod.

"Did you think I poisoned your food?"

"No."

"Then why didn't you eat it?" I push.

"I thought you might've drugged it."

My brows almost reach my hairline. "Drugged it?"

"Wouldn't be the first time."

"Did Sei drug you?" I demand.

With another jerky nod, she drops her gaze to her lap.

"Why would he drug you if you were already kidnapped? What's the point?" I wonder aloud.

Her dry laugh is haunting as she answers, "To see my face when I woke up in my own blood the first time."

36

Nauseated, I drop the subject, positive that if I hear another word, I'll find a way to get Sei out of prison just so I can gut him the way he deserves. Keeping my expression indifferent, I announce, "The housekeeper dropped off a bag of clothes that should fit you. Get dressed in something comfortable and come downstairs."

"Why?"

"Because we're going to teach you how to defend yourself."

She rolls her eyes, giving me a glimpse of the sassy woman she was before she was kidnapped.

"That won't be necessary," she deflects.

"Why not?"

"Because no matter how much you kick, scream, bite, and scratch, they always win. *Always*. Trust me. I've been there."

My astonishment is palpable as I stare at the broken girl in front of me. The one that accepts her shitty past, practically embracing it to become her future. And it pisses me off.

"Were you always this weak?" I snap.

Her jaw drops. "Excuse me?"

"I want to know."

"How dare you—"

"No. How dare you," I spit, my frustration boiling over. "Fuck Sei. Fuck what he did to you. And fuck all those memories that haunt you at night. But the sick bastard doesn't have to win. That's still within your power. Even if he held you down and raped you right here on this floor, he couldn't take your strength and your fight unless you gave it to him. Unless you let him win. That choice is still up to you."

"Screw you, D. You don't know what I've been through—"

"You're right. I don't. And even the little glimpses you've given me have gutted me, Q. But the second I try to give you back an ounce of the power he stole from you, you push it away. Like it wouldn't have made a difference. Like you've

37

already given in. Hell, you won't even look in the mirror, you're so ashamed."

"Can you blame me? He used me. Tortured me. Chewed me up, then spit me out." Her voice cracks as she clutches at the pillow tucked against her chest, desperate to end this conversation. But I refuse to let her off that easily.

"Don't you hear yourself?" I growl. "*He* did those things. *Sei.* Not you. You have nothing to be ashamed of."

"Bullshit," she starts, her face red with anger and shame.

"Stop," I order her. "Stop blaming yourself."

Her pain is suffocating as she drops her head back to the headboard behind her and cries, "How can I? If what you're saying is true, then I let it happen. I didn't fight hard enough."

"Screw that. You endured something, Q. Something no one should ever have to endure. But I need you to understand that he didn't just break your body. He broke your mind. Your willpower. Everything. And I can't sit by and watch that happen. I can't let your bitterness consume you until there's nothing left. It's your choice to fight for your future. To get it back. To *not* let him win. Despite his best efforts, he doesn't own you. I just need you to believe that too."

"And if I can't?" she challenges.

"Then you're letting the bastard win." Storming out of her bedroom, I slam the door behind me then rush down the stairs to Matteo's gym on the first floor.

But it does nothing to douse the rage licking at my soul.

6

Q

The bed is soft and doesn't smell like urine. It's the main piece of evidence I have that I'm not in that dank basement anymore, and I cling to it like my life depends on it. Rolling onto my side, I breathe deep and let the scent of freshly-washed sheets ground me. I've been here for a little while now, but the clean smell never gets old.

I haven't talked to D since breakfast, but that hasn't stopped his words from playing on a constant loop in my mind. I'm still pissed at him. For the things he said. For the crap he knows nothing about. And for making me question my own decisions and how the hell I'm supposed to move forward.

Maybe he's right. Maybe I always have been this weak. Maybe I'm not willing to fight for a shitty future when I don't even know what it would look like with a girl as broken as me.

There's a quiet knock at the door. My pulse jumps before the scent of the cotton brings me back to the present.

I'm not in Sei's custody anymore. He can't hurt me here.

But is that really true? Because I'm still hurting. Bad. I can still feel his touch against my skin. I can still hear his voice and the way it would crack when he was excited. I can still smell his rancid breath laced with cigarette smoke and alcohol.

Even though my body has escaped, my mind is still in his prison.

And I hate him for it.

Another quiet knock distracts me, yanking me back to the present.

"Hey, Blue?" D calls from the hallway.

He might not be able to see me from the half-opened door, but he knows I'm in here. Where else would I be? And why the hell did he call me Blue? I just want to lay in bed and zone out in front of a TV. Or at least, that's what the old me would've done.

Now, I'm not sure how I should spend my time when I'm not dreading the seconds that tick by, bringing me closer to another visit from Sei.

He's gone, I remind myself. *He's in prison. He can't hurt me anymore.*

"Blue?" D tries again. "You in there?"

"Of course, I'm in here. Where else would I go?" I mutter under my breath while ignoring the fact that he has the decency not to snoop into my personal space even though my door is partially open.

"Q?" he calls.

Holding on to the familiarity of his voice, I force myself to stand, then pad over to the door.

"Hey," he mutters when I come into view.

I lean my head against the doorjamb and wait for him to continue.

What the hell do you want, asshole?

"You hungry?"

My stomach grumbles at the mention of food, causing D's

mouth to quirk up in amusement. "I take that as a yes. There's lasagna in the oven. It'll be ready any minute."

"You cooked?" The question slips out of me before I can stop it.

Keep your mouth shut, Q! a tiny voice inside of me yells.

But for some reason, Diece seems to make the one thing I learned when in captivity surprisingly difficult. Actually, he makes a lot of things difficult. Like forcing me to acknowledge my pain so that one day I can try to heal from it instead of letting myself drown in it.

And I'm tired of fighting to keep my head above water.

"Nah," he returns before running his fingers through his dark, wavy hair, completely oblivious to my inner dialogue. "The housekeeper has a bunch of frozen food prepared in the freezer. I just have to put it in the oven."

"Oh."

"You should come downstairs and eat."

Look at that. Another command.

On your knees and open your mouth. You bite me, I cut out your tongue.

I dig my teeth into the inside of my cheek until the tang of blood seeps onto my taste buds. With a slow, deliberate blink, I obey Diece's command and step into the hallway with my attention glued to the carpet. His big, burly body stops me in my tracks.

"Stop."

I freeze.

"I'm not your prison guard, Q."

Sure, you're not, I think to myself, but I don't say a word.

"Look at me."

I drag my gaze from the floor and meet his intense stare. He has handsome eyes. They're framed with dark lashes, but the color is something else. Like melted chocolate with a few swirls of caramel. But it's the warmth that really does me in.

"I don't own you," he growls. "You could walk out that door right now if you wanted, and I wouldn't stop you."

The warmth dissipates as I'm reminded, yet again, where I land on the damn totem pole.

At the very bottom.

My eyes burn with hatred, but I bite my tongue to keep from arguing with him. Still, the bastard can read me like a book. "I'm serious, Q. You're here because you saved our asses during Burlone's tournament. I've already told you this. We're trying to protect you. But if you're unhappy and think you'd have more luck at surviving on your own, then I won't make you stay. Understand?"

With my lips pulled into a thin line, I don't bother to reply but wait for his next request. Because they always want more from me.

His Adam's apple bobs up and down before another growl of frustration slips out of him. "I'm not the enemy, Q."

"Sure, you're not," I seethe, losing the battle against my own self-control.

Jaw clenching and nostrils flaring, he takes a deep breath and searches for an ounce of patience. "Do you want to talk about it? Is that what you want? Do you want me to leave you alone? Do you want me to drop you off somewhere? Deliver your food to your room? What. Do. You. Want?" His breath fans across my face as I find myself standing chest to chest with the bear in front of me.

"You wanna know what I want?" I spit.

"Yeah. I do."

"Fine. I want to think for myself. I want to *not* be broken. I want to know what it's like to have someone touch me without feeling like spiders are crawling along my skin. I want to be the girl I was before I was kidnapped. I want to be strong. I want to be fearless. And I want to disappear because I know I'll never get any of those things back. Sei took them from me. All of it. And now, I'm just a shell of a human being, yet you're asking me to be more than that."

"I'm asking you to face your fears," he counters.

"And if I can't do that?"

"Then you can stay in your room and let what's left of your life pass you by."

"Fine," I spit. "If you don't own me, then that's exactly what you're going to let me do."

"Fine." He stares me down, waiting for my next move, and even though it kills me inside, I step back and reach for the door so I can slam it in his face. My grip tightens against the heavy wood as my own self-loathing threatens to consume me. Because I can't even slam a freaking door without drowning in my past.

A high-pitched scream claws its way up my throat before I slam the door in the opposite direction. Over and over again. The hinges groan in protest at the odd angle as the handle leaves a small scar in the drywall. Then I slide onto my butt and cry.

I'm so freaking broken.

"Q—"

"Just leave me alone," I beg with my head in my hands. I can feel him watching me. "Go!"

The floor creaks as he walks away.

And all I'm left with is guilt.

He doesn't deserve to be treated like shit. But he doesn't get it. He doesn't understand.

Or maybe he refuses to let me self-destruct the way I desperately want to.

A few minutes later, another soft knock echoes throughout the room. The hallway is empty except for a square of lasagna resting on a plate. It smells delicious, but it seems I've lost my appetite.

7

Q

I spend the next day in my room, unsure if I'm really allowed to explore the premises or if it's a trap so Diece can have an excuse to punish me. A soft knock greets me in the evening, but when I dig up the courage to approach the hallway, only a plate of pasta can be found. Despite the flavorful marinara, it turns to sawdust as soon as it touches my tongue while my conversations with Diece play on a constant loop in my mind.

I really am weak. I'm letting Sei win. But how does he expect me to just...let my past go? Especially after everything I've been through. I can't do that. But I also can't drown in this hate anymore. It's killing me.

And so are the nightmares.

"Please. Please, Sei. Don't—"

"Come on, my pretty Peach. You love this game."

"I-I don't," I cry, squirming away from him. *"I don't love it—"*

"Then we'll play it until you do."

I wake up in a cold sweat, tangled in my sheets, as another sob escapes me.

Just a dream, Q. It's just a dream, I remind myself, but it doesn't make the feel of his knife scraping against my inner thighs go away.

Angrily, I wipe away the tears that stain my cheeks before my senses prickle with awareness. With my breath caught in my lungs, I scan the dark room and find a shadowed figure resting against the wall with a gun in his hand. My terror spikes before the moonlight from the window kisses his handsome features.

It's Diece.

"W-what are you doing here?" My voice is rusty from sleep. Or maybe it's from my screams. Regardless, I watch him carefully and wait for his response. He looks tired. Worn down. Like he hasn't slept in weeks.

His sigh is filled with a sadness that makes my chest ache. But there isn't resentment or pity that weaves its way into his resignation. Just…sadness.

For me.

For what I've been through.

For the nightmares that won't go away.

"Get some sleep, Q," he tells me before resting his head against the wall behind him. "I won't let the monsters get you."

Digging my teeth into my lower lip, I continue to study him for a few more seconds. If he wanted to kill me, he would've already done it. I roll onto my side and give him my back, squeezing the pillow against my chest as tight as I can. Then I close my eyes and pray for sleep.

And for some reason, it comes easier with the knowledge that I'm not alone.

Though I refuse to acknowledge why.

THE NEXT MORNING, MY ROOM IS MISSING A CERTAIN protector, and I start to question whether or not I imagined his presence last night. I did sleep better, though. Not perfect. But...still. Sei remained present to haunt my dreams, but I couldn't feel his touch this time, so I guess that's progress.

It's late. Later than normal, anyway. D hasn't knocked on my door yet. Or maybe I slept through it? With my arms folded across my chest, I peek through my open doorway and scan the hall. It's empty. No plate of bacon and eggs. No glass of juice. Nothing. Curious, I rock back on my heels before finding the courage to explore my new prison more fully. My anxiety heightens as my bare feet pad against the dark wood floor. Creeping down the stairs, I wait for someone to yell at me or grab me and shove me back to my room. But no one does.

What if...what if something happened to D? What if that's why he didn't bring me breakfast? What if he's hurt? What if Sei found me and killed him? The questions run rampant on my frazzled nerves, begging me to hide away in my room, but I restrain myself.

I need to find Diece.

Closing my eyes, I focus on the sounds around me, but the place is practically silent. My ears perk when I recognize an almost familiar song filtering from down the hall. It's so quiet, I'm surprised I can hear it, but I tiptoe toward it in hopes of finding D. The door is cracked open a few inches, and I peek through it.

With a quiet gasp, I take in a very ripped backside as my protector from the night before pummels a punching bag. Black basketball shorts hang low on his hips, but his top half is bare and glistens from the sweat clinging to his olive skin. His muscles ripple and flex with every swing of his arm, leaving my mouth watering at the sight. "Ain't No Rest For

The Wicked" by Cage the Elephant blares through the speakers. With the force of a Mack truck, he delivers a final right hook that makes the punching bag jerk back. As if he can feel my stare, he glances over his shoulder. His gaze pierces me with its intensity.

"Morning," he grunts.

It's like my veins were injected with slurry concrete. I can't move a muscle. I can't escape. Part of me feels like I've been caught with my hand in the proverbial cookie jar. But...what now?

Holding my attention hostage, his tongue darts out between his lips, then he stalks closer to me. My entire body buzzes with anticipation, though I'm not sure why. His moves are deliberate. Precise. Proving he has more control over every single ounce of muscle clinging to his bones than a freaking panther, even though he looks like a damn grizzly. When he's less than a foot away from me, my nose tickles with awareness as his scent filters through the air. He smells amazing, and I have to fight the urge to lean closer and take a deep breath. It doesn't stop my mouth from watering, though. His giant hand reaches forward, and I'm convinced he's going to tug me into him until I notice the small towel rack placed right next to the entrance.

Grabbing one of the towels, he wipes the sweat from his brow, then slowly grasps the edge of the door and pushes it open the rest of the way.

"I said, good morning," he repeats.

I swallow thickly. "Morning."

"You're out of your room."

"Someone forgot to bring me breakfast."

With a flash of his boyish grin I'm slowly becoming accustomed to, he grabs the back of his neck and squeezes. "Sorry, Blue. During our conversation yesterday, I realized something."

"And what's that?"

"I've been enabling you."

I flinch back. "What's that supposed to mean? And why did you call me Blue?"

"The hair." I can almost feel his eyes caress my messy, short locks before he adds, "The emotions."

"Emotions?"

"You know...you've been feeling blue."

"So, my real name isn't acceptable now? You needed to come up with a nickname?"

He rolls his eyes. "Not what I meant, but if we're on the topic, I might as well ask you something. No one has filled out a missing person's report for anyone by the name of Queena. Do you know why that would be, Blue?"

I shrug one shoulder but stay silent.

"Don't escape on me now," he pushes before gently tapping his index finger against my temple. "You get lost up here too often, Q. Stay with me for a little longer, yeah?"

I remain quiet but hold his gaze when I desperately want to close my eyes and ignore the way my heart races anytime he's near.

"Who are you, Q?"

"No one."

"I don't believe that for one second."

"You should."

"Why?"

"Because it's the truth. No one filled out a report because no one misses me. I'm no one."

"And I disagree," he returns. "You hungry?"

A small part of me is begging to be stubborn and deny it, but I'm too hungry to follow through. Instead, I give him a grudging nod.

"Let's get you some food." He slips past me, but not before his chest brushes against mine. With my breath caught in my lungs, I wait for the feeling of disgust to fill me at the contact, but it doesn't appear. And neither does my fear.

Tucking away that little insight for later, I follow him to the kitchen. It's decorated with the same rich red accents, gold sconces, and patterned fleur-de-lis wallpaper that matches the rest of the house. Eggs are cracking within minutes as a comfortable silence envelops the room. Once they're placed on some ceramic plates, he sets one in front of me then plops down onto one of the barstools. "How'd you sleep?"

"Better." I take a bite of the freshly scrambled eggs and almost moan. I was so used to living off cold broth and tepid water that I'd almost forgotten what good food tastes like. And even the meals that I've had since arriving here haven't held a candle to these, although I refuse to admit it's because I'm eating them at an actual counter with company instead of cross-legged on the floor all by myself.

Again, I can feel Diece watching me, but it doesn't have the same creepy-crawly feeling I'd grown accustomed to when Sei was around.

Which reminds me....

Before I can talk myself out of it, I glance over at him. "Thank you, by the way."

"For what?"

"For staying with me last night. I'm sure the floor isn't comfortable, but...." I push around a bit of the egg on my plate. "I felt better knowing I wasn't alone."

He nods before taking a bite of his breakfast. After he chews and swallows, he sets down his fork. "I know this is going to take time for you to accept, but not everyone is like Sei. Even in this business," he adds with a defeated smirk. "Sei was the scum of the earth, and if he wasn't already in custody, I'd kill him for you."

Chewing on my lower lip, I tear my gaze from his and

shove another bite of breakfast into my mouth. But the flavor was ruined as soon as *his* name was mentioned.

"I'm sorry I've been an ass," Diece continues.

"I'm sorry I've been emotional," I return with a shy smile.

"You're allowed to be emotional. You're allowed to be whatever the hell you want."

I snort. "Sure, I am."

"So...have you considered my proposition?"

"About what?"

"Learning to defend yourself."

Oh. *That.*

"I uh," I hesitate, searching for the right words that won't turn our conversation into another argument. "I don't know how much it'll really help."

"Well, it definitely wouldn't hurt," he counters. "Besides, it's not like we're doing much around here anyway. Aren't you bored?"

"Maybe." I look around the vast kitchen to avoid his gaze.

"Then look at it that way. It's something to fill the time until Kingston says it's safe to come out of hiding."

Another bite of eggs fills my mouth as I weigh the pros and cons before swallowing it down.

"You might even have fun," he prods, sensing how close I am to caving.

I roll my eyes. "Fine."

"Yeah?"

His disbelief makes me want to laugh, but I hold it in. "Yeah. I'll do it."

"Good." His playful tone turns ominous as he leans forward and adds, "There's one condition, though."

"What's that?"

"I'm going to have to touch you, Q."

I shake my head. "I can't—"

"I know. I know it'll be hard."

"You don't understand—"

"I know," he repeats, gently. "I know I don't get it. I know that even if you sat me down and explained all the shit you went through with explicit detail, it still wouldn't make me fully understand. But if you want to get past this, then you need to try. And you need to trust someone to help you."

Staring at the cold eggs in front of me, I try not to get lost in my memories, but it's so. Damn. *Hard*. "I'm not sure I know what trust is anymore."

"I get that." He bumps his shoulder against mine. "But, you gotta try."

The thought of him touching me—of anyone touching me—is torture. But the possibility of learning how to defend myself is so damn tempting that I'm desperate to reach out and grab hold of it. I'd give anything to feel powerful. Strong. Hell, pretty much anything that doesn't include self-loathing and…dirty.

"Okay. I'll try," I whisper while hating the way my stomach feels like it's been knotted inside of me.

"I won't let you down," he promises. "Go change. I'm gonna grab a quick shower. Then we'll get to work."

"Right now?" I ask with wide eyes.

"Yeah. No time like the present, right?" That same crooked smile makes my heart gallop before he stands up and strides toward the second floor, where I assume he's going to shower.

With a gulp, I put our plates in the sink.

Well. Alright then.

8

DIECE

With a sour look, I glare at the gray T-shirt folded on the bathroom counter before slipping it over my head. I'm not used to exercising in anything other than a pair of shorts, but I don't want her to think I'm doing this for anything sexual, and it's going to be hard enough not to get a fucking erection with her touching my chest when we brawl.

This was a bad idea.

After I slide on my dark-red joggers, I head across the hall and knock on Blue's partially opened door, but she doesn't answer.

"Hey, Blue?" I call out.

Silence.

"Blue?"

After another thirty seconds of silence, I jog down the stairs toward the gym. The door is cracked, and the rhythmic sound of exercise equipment confirms my suspicion. With a soft push, I open the door the rest of the way, but my steps falter when I find Q sprinting at full speed on the treadmill. Her tits are bouncing up and down as her feet pound against the machine with sweat dripping down her forehead. She's lost in her own world, completely oblivious to my presence, and finally losing herself in something beneficial for her health—both mentally and physically.

About damn time.

Mesmerized, I watch her pouty lips form a small 'o' as she releases the oxygen from her lungs, continuing to focus on the wall in front of her before she picks up her pace.

She's gorgeous.

Blinking, I shove aside the imagery and stride over to her.

"You were a runner before." It isn't a question. Her long strides and even breathing are the only evidence I need.

Her gaze shoots to mine before returning to the blank wall as she keeps up her steady rhythm.

"You can come down here whenever you want. You know that, right? Even if we aren't training."

She stays quiet but pushes the red button to stop the treadmill from moving. Then she steps off and stands in front of me, silently waiting for my instruction.

Freedom scares her now. I can see it in her eyes, can feel it in her hesitant movements any time I ask something of her. Like she can't quite figure out how to act on her own without someone telling her what to do.

Shaking off the messed-up realization, I announce, "We're going to start with some hand-to-hand defense. Come over to the mat with me."

She follows without a word but folds her arms across her ample chest and keeps her attention glued to the blue mats beneath our feet as soon as we reach it. She's nervous. I can feel it. Hell, I can almost taste it. But she's here. She's at least *trying* to trust someone. To trust *me*. And that's all that matters. The pad of my finger brushes beneath her chin as I force her to look up at me. When our eyes connect, she gulps, and I drop my hand back down to my side.

"How're you feeling?"

With a one-shouldered shrug, she looks back at the ground.

Come on, Blue. Stay with me.

Rocking back on my heels, I ask, "Have you ever heard of a safe word?"

She shakes her head, then peeks back up at me.

"It's a word that tells me to stop. When you say this word, I do exactly that. I stop. No matter what. No matter the position. I *stop*," I reiterate. "We clear?"

Her entire body trembles, but I doubt she even recognizes it as she whispers, "What's the word?"

"Whatever you want it to be. Hell, it can be *stop* for all I care, but you need to understand the power of that word and that I won't ever push you to go any further if you say it."

Chewing on her lower lip, she hesitates before stammering, "Six."

"Six?"

"Yeah."

"Why six?"

"Sei in Italian is six." Her voice is barely above a whisper.

It takes everything inside of me to keep my expression neutral when I feel like I just got kicked in the stomach. "Okay. Six it is. Ready to start?"

Her breath is shallow, but she forces herself to nod.

"Okay. I want to see where your instincts take you, so I'm going to grab you from behind. I want you to try to get me off you, then run away. You're fast. If you can break free, then you can get away from your attacker."

"So you're telling me that I just need to…run away?" If she weren't so terrified right now, I'd almost think she was making fun of me.

"You don't want to fight with your attacker because when

it comes to brute strength, you'll rarely come out ahead," I explain. "Does that make sense?"

"Oh. Yes. That makes sense."

"And what's your safe word?"

"S-six," she stutters.

Grabbing her face, I make her look me straight in the eye. "I'm not going to hurt you, Q. I promise. You say six, and I'm off you in a second. Understand?"

Her lower lip quivers, but she nods in my grasp, and I've never been more proud. This girl is braver than she thinks. I just need to make her believe it.

I release my hold and drop my hands back down to my sides, then slowly circle her. "Good. Let's do this."

When I'm behind her, I pull her into a bear hug, wrapping my arms around her torso and beneath her arms. But she doesn't move a damn muscle. It's as if my touch has the power to completely disarm her, yet I haven't even done anything.

"Q," I growl. "Fight me."

Her chest rises and falls in an unsteady pattern. I squeeze her tighter and force out, "I said, fight me, Q. *Now.*"

She's paralyzed.

Releasing my hold, I make her face me before leaning closer until all she can see is my ugly mug a few inches from her gorgeous, terrified face. "Look at me, Q."

A spark ignites inside of her as she holds my stare.

"Fight me. I want you to kick and scream. I want you to fucking claw my eyes out. I want you to try. Do you think you can do that for me?"

"I–I don't know," she stutters.

"Can you try? Please?"

Her breath is staggered as she releases all the pent-up oxygen in her lungs before giving me a jerky nod. "I'll try."

"And if you can't take it—"

55

"I say my safe word," she snaps. "I get it."

"Good girl."

Pulling her into another bear hug from behind, I snake my arms around her ribcage, then raise her a few inches into the air and yell, "Fight!"

She wiggles against me, kicking and screaming, but it does nothing to stop me from dragging her wherever the hell I feel like taking her.

After a few seconds of struggling, I let her go and step away to give her a minute to breathe. She's seconds from a panic attack, but my chest swells with pride at the knowledge that she didn't use her safe word. She stayed strong.

"That was good," I acknowledge, though I'm lying through my teeth. "But it wasn't enough to stop me from doing whatever the hell I wanted."

"I know."

"I'm going to grab you again, but this time I want you to listen to what I'm saying, then follow my instructions, and we'll see if we can get you out of that hold. Understand?"

With another jerky nod, she gives me her back and waits.

Pulling her against my chest, I keep my grip tight but not suffocating. "If you're in this position, you want to try to headbutt me with the back of your head. Aim for my nose and forehead. If your hit connects, it'll disorient your attacker, and their grip will loosen, giving you the chance to twist out of their grasp and get away. If your hit doesn't connect the way you want it to, squat low and use your weight against them before trying to headbutt them again. It's a lot harder to hold on to something that's using gravity and their full body weight to keep them in place instead of doing half the work for them with your own legs. Does that make sense?"

Her hair tickles my chin as she nods against me. Ignoring the way she feels in my arms, I murmur, "Okay.

Don't headbutt me, but try squatting low and making your-self heavier."

She does, and my muscles protest from the added weight. "Good. Now twist your torso and aim that elbow at my face. You want to hit over and over again. It'll take more than one hit to get them to let you go, but you can do it."

We practice this position a few more times before moving on to the one I fear has been used against her multiple times.

"How do you feel?" I ask.

"Good, I guess?"

"You guess?" I laugh.

With her hands on her hips and her skin drenched in sweat, she grimaces. "Yes?"

Another chuckle escapes me before I let her off the hook. "I guess that's progress. Now we're gonna talk about when he would grab your hair to keep you in place."

The comment makes her freeze as she gets lost in her nightmares. All it took was mentioning him once, and she's spiraling.

Closing the distance between us, I cup her cheek. "Stay with me, Blue."

She sniffs then nods, coming back to the present.

"When would he pull your hair?" My voice is quiet.

She gulps, but her gaze stays hazy as she battles the memories waging war inside of her.

"Answer me, Blue."

"When he'd want to keep me in place so that I couldn't get away from him. Sometimes it was on the floor. Sometimes on the bed."

Nostrils flaring, I clear my throat and shove aside my rage that doesn't belong in this room. It belongs in Sei's prison cell.

"Okay," I breathe. "I want to practice that position, but I need you to trust me."

"D...." Her voice trails off as her fear threatens to choke her.

"If you don't know how to get out of that position, then it'll always be your worst nightmare. Let me teach you how. Do you trust me?"

Her lips pull into a thin line as she stares back at me with an intensity that almost breaks me. But I'm not going to push her on this. Not if she isn't ready. Nostrils flaring, she rolls onto her back, then looks up at me, waiting for me to get into position without saying a word. It's another test. Another chance for me to be the guy she fears I am. But she's doing it anyway, despite the possibility that I could be like Sei.

Squatting low, I ask her, "What's your safe word, Q?"

"Six."

"Say it again."

"Six," she says with a bit more confidence.

"Good girl." Straddling her hips, I tangle my fingers in her short blue hair but keep my grip loose in hopes that she can focus and won't be triggered. "You okay?"

"Six," she breathes, squeezing her eyes shut before I can even voice my question.

I climb off her as fast as I can, then raise my hands in the air. "I'm off. I'm off."

That same ragged breathing echoes throughout the room as she rolls onto her side and tucks her knees into her chest. "I'm...I'm sorry."

"Don't be sorry. You did good. You faced your fears—"

"I didn't face it—"

"You *tried*, Q. That's all I care about. Let's focus on some other ways you can defend yourself, okay?"

Offering my hand, I wait for her to take it, and by some miracle, she does.

I think I passed.

Again and again, we practice different techniques until she's confident she can get out of his grasp or break his arm with a few moves that transform from complicated to second nature. But never when she's on her back. And I don't blame her. One day though, she'll have to face her fears again. But not today.

With our chests heaving, I fall onto my ass and praise her. "You did good today."

She smiles but doesn't reply.

"Seriously, Blue. Tomorrow we'll go over these moves again. Then we'll move onto weapons."

"Weapons?"

"Yeah. Sometimes it isn't just hand-to-hand defense. Did he use a gun to threaten you? A knife? What makes you feel helpless? Vulnerable?"

A glassy film spreads across her eyes as she gets lost in another memory, making me hate the asshole even more than before. I feel like we've made so much progress today, but it can fall apart in the blink of an eye.

Frustrated, I snap my fingers in front of her. "Focus, Blue. Where'd you go?"

She clears her throat. "A knife. He liked his knives."

"Then we'll teach you how to use one against him," I promise her. "But not today. Go shower. I'll make dinner, and we can watch a show or something."

"A show?"

I laugh. "Yeah. Is that a problem?"

"No," she admits, but her cheeks heat with embarrassment as she drops her gaze to the ground like a shy little kitten.

"Then why are you blushing?" I tease. There's just something about this girl that makes me desperate to knock down the barrier she's constructed around herself, though I doubt she'll ever let me get close enough to try.

"I just"—she tucks a few strands of hair behind her ear —"didn't picture you doing something so…normal."

"Why not?"

"Because you're a big, bad mafia man?" she offers.

"And that means I can't enjoy a show every once in a while?"

"I dunno? I thought being part of the mob is a lifestyle choice, not a job," she quips, giving me another glimpse of the old Q. "Am I wrong?"

"It is, but everyone needs some time to unwind and shit. How do you like to unwind?"

Aaand there's the damn barrier again.

I can almost see it rise up a few more levels as I ask a question that apparently is too personal for her own liking. She chews her lower lip and suddenly finds an unhealthy fascination with the stained concrete beneath our feet that covers the entire gym area while ignoring me completely.

"Blue?" I prod.

"Just shows and stuff."

"What kind of shows?"

"Depends on the time of year."

"For example…?" I let my voice trail off in hopes that she'll throw me a bone and fill in the blank.

"Like Christmastime."

"And?" I press. It's like every damn conversation turns into an interrogation with her.

"And watching the Hallmark Channel?"

"Like the sappy love shit?"

That same blush spreads from her cheeks out to her ears and down her neck, and I bite back my laughter at how uncomfortable this conversation is making her.

"It's stupid." She tries to step around me, but I grab her bicep and keep her in place.

"It's not stupid. I'm just…surprised."

Her attention is glued to my hand encompassing her arm. "Why is that so surprising?"

"Because it's so...normal for someone like you."

"Someone like me?" Her gaze darts up to mine and damn near acts like a microscope on my soul. Like a switch has been flipped, she lifts her chin and spits, "Someone who was kidnapped, raped, and tortured? Is that what you mean?"

"What?" With my hands raised in surrender, I attempt to defuse the situation. "That's not what I meant—"

"Then what did you mean?"

"The first personal thing I've learned about you is that you like Hallmark movies. You've kept everything else in the dark, and anytime I've tried to pry, you've ignored me completely or clammed up, making me feel guilty as hell for asking in the first place."

"That's because I'm not anyone special, D. I'm just a normal girl who was in the wrong place at the wrong time."

"And where were you? When you were taken?" I push.

"It doesn't matter—"

"Maybe it does."

"No. It doesn't. Because the girl from my past is long gone. She disappeared the moment I was kidnapped, held down, and fucked in the ass, okay?" Wrenching herself out of my grasp, she storms off to shower. Her march is fueled with animosity as she disappears around the corner and leaves me alone with my guilt over a crime I didn't even commit.

What the hell just happened?

Pinching the bridge of my nose, I dial Lou.

"Yeah?"

"Hey," I reply. "I need you to do me a favor."

"What kind of favor?"

"I need you to download as many Hallmark movies as you can, then send them over to me."

"Hallmark movies?" Lou questions. I can almost see his

look of confusion.

"Yeah," I grit out. "The Christmas ones. Think you can do that for me?"

After a slight pause, he returns, "Sure thing. Anything else?"

"That's it. Do we have any updates on the families? Anyone looking for her?"

"King asked Dex to take care of the buyer who'd been set up to purchase Q after the tournament, but other than that, it's been pretty silent."

My knuckles tighten around my phone as I press it against my ear. What kind of prick would buy a girl instead of just finding one like a normal human being?

With a heavy exhale, I switch the lights off in the gym, then head to my room. "Alright. Thanks."

"No problem. How's it going down there?"

I take the stairs two at a time, then glance over at Q's door. A few inches keep it from being closed entirely, proving that she's still more terrified of being locked in than she is of sacrificing an ounce of privacy. Which means she still doesn't trust me.

"As good as can be expected, I guess," I grumble under my breath.

"Is she giving you any trouble?"

"Nothing I can't handle."

"Sounds good. I'll upload the movies to Matteo's online theater system as soon as they're ready. You should be able to play them on any of the TVs connected to his internet."

"Thanks."

"Don't mention it."

Then I hang up and take a hot shower, while the haunted look in Q's eyes plagues me. She's so hot then cold that I don't know how to handle her, and it's slowly chipping away at my sanity.

9

Q

I'm fuming. I have been for the past forty-five minutes. Pretty sure the lush carpet beneath my bare feet is going to get track marks if I keep this pacing up for much longer, but I can't help it. Something about his comment pissed me off.

It made me miss the old me. Gave me an inkling of what it felt like to feel normal before realizing it was ripped away from me and left me spiraling out of control with no identity and no idea how to move forward.

Knock, knock.

Chewing on my lower lip, I stare at the piece of solid oak that I can't make myself close before marching toward it and wrenching the damn thing the rest of the way open.

"Dinner's ready," D announces as if our little confrontation from earlier didn't even happen. But maybe that's how mafia men settle their arguments when they can't shoot someone to get their way. By pretending they never happened in the first place.

His hair is still wet from his shower, and I have to fight the urge to reach out and touch it. He just looks so...*human* right now. So normal. So *not* like the big bad mafia bear I've grown accustomed to. My heart continues its frantic pace but for an entirely different reason that I refuse to acknowledge.

"Would you like to come downstairs and eat it with me?" he prods. It's a request, not a demand. Grudgingly, I acknowledge his effort to make me feel comfortable but can't decide what to actually do about it.

"Please?" he adds before tacking on a crooked smirk that would've made the old me melt into a puddle at his feet.

I would've been a shy mess around him before I was taken. I would've probably run in the opposite direction because the guy oozes sex, confidence, and bad decisions. But that wouldn't have stopped me from crushing on him from a distance. He just...has this charisma that could be so addictive if I allowed myself to taste it.

But the new me would never do that, and the old me would've been too terrified by his bad boy demeanor to try.

"Come on, Blue. It'll be fun. I might even have a surprise for you."

"I don't like surprises. Not anymore."

"You'll like this one. I promise."

I used to love surprises. Now, I'm not so sure anymore. But it's the pleading in his gaze that finally does me in and convinces me to step into the hallway.

I bite the inside of my cheek and mutter, "Fine."

His eyes flash with surprise before he covers it with a warm smile. "Perfect."

The silence is deafening as we walk down to the kitchen, where a white paper bag is resting on the counter. He grabs it but keeps walking. "Follow me."

Leading me down a winding hall on the main floor, then down a set of stairs into the basement, he opens a door on his right and motions to the dark room. My heart rate is off the charts, but I try to calm the hell down as I take in the space.

It's a theater room. There's a large screen on one wall with a projector hanging in the center of the ceiling and a few rows of recliner chairs and loveseats placed on ascending platforms to the back of the room.

It's...legit.

Licking my lips, I scan the area a few more times to remind myself that this basement is literally nothing like the one I was imprisoned in. Well, other than the fact that it's in the basement.

"You okay?" I can feel him inspecting me, watching me to see if I'm about to snap and lose my damn mind more than I already have. And the fact that he's already learning to anticipate my mental breakdowns is...depressing. And a little impressive. He might even know me better than myself.

With a sniff, I take a deep breath and face him. "Yup. Fine."

He doesn't believe me but also doesn't press the subject, and I'm grateful he's willing to drop it.

"Alright, then. There's a fridge over there." He points to the giant wall with the white screen. A fridge is tucked beside it. "Grab me a water, will ya? I'll turn the projector on. Then we'll start the movie."

The sleek, stainless steel appliance is a stark reminder of the opulence in this house. When I open it, my hand itches to grab a Coke, but I reach for a second bottle of water before closing it and taking a seat on the nearest leather recliner. My muscles practically melt into the cushions on impact, and a contented sigh slips out of me. I'm exhausted. But it's a good exhaustion. One that reminds me of the productive day I had instead of wasting away in a locked room.

The screen goes bright seconds later before Christmas music filters through the speakers.

What the hell?

Convinced I'm seeing things, I blink a few times before digging my teeth into my lower lip to keep from crying. White paper bag in hand, Diece plops down beside me and rummages through it. He's completely oblivious that I'm about to *really* lose my shit for the first time since I was kidnapped.

"Hey, Blue," he starts as he pulls out a hamburger wrapped in aluminum foil. "I didn't know what you like, so I just got—" His expression transforms from carefree to distressed in an instant as he glances over at me. "What the hell, Blue? What's wrong?"

My body wracks with a sob as I bury my face in my hands. Gasping for air, I finally just...cry. For the girl I was. For everything I've been through. For every bruise. Every cut. Every moment that was stolen from me by the despicable monster who tortured me for two weeks that lasted longer than a lifetime.

A hand rubs against my back, but I jerk away from the foreign touch of comfort and cry even harder before those same strong hands pull me into a warm chest. Unable to fight it, I cling to his comfort and sob even harder. The worn cotton shirt feels soft against my cheek as I burrow into him. I don't know how much time passes before his chest rumbles against my cheek.

"Shhh...it's okay, Q. It's gonna be okay."

I shake my head back and forth as another cry escapes me. "No, it's not. It'll never be okay again. I hate him, D. I hate him so much."

"I know, baby girl," he coos. "I know."

"I'm sorry. I'm so sorry," I choke out as my sorrow threatens to swallow me whole.

His grip tightens around me until all I can feel, smell, and hear is him. "Don't you dare be sorry, Q. Not for one fucking second. You have done nothing wrong, do you hear me? Nothing."

"I'm broken. I let him use me—"

"You had no choice," he argues. His tone is dripping with venom. "You did what you had to do to survive. And you *did* survive, Q. You made it out the other side. That's more than most girls can say. I know it doesn't feel like it, but you're strong enough to get through this."

I whimper. "I'm not, though. I'm not strong. You were right. I'm weak. I let him win."

"Don't you dare let yourself think that, Blue. I was wrong. When I told you that, I was *wrong*. You got up this morning. You faced the world, despite how dark it seems. You're here. You showed up. You did more than most men or women ever could. You are strong. You are brave. And you're gonna get through this."

"And if I can't?"

"Then I'll do whatever I can to carry your burdens until you're strong enough to take the weight again."

With tear-stained cheeks, I peek up at him, positive I look like a mess, yet feeling almost clean for the first time since I woke up in that damn basement all those nights ago.

His hand almost engulfs the entire left side of my face as he rubs his thumb along my cheek, catching the moisture still clinging to my skin. The indecision is clear in his eyes. If only I knew what he was thinking about. My lips part. But I don't move another muscle as I continue to hold his stare. The air is heavy around us while the forgotten movie dances along the screen. I lift my chin. Hold my breath. And—

Defeated, he drops his hand back to his side and finds my cold hamburger before offering it to me. "You should eat something."

"Thanks." I take it from him and unwrap it while my brain tries to piece together what the hell just happened.

"Have you seen this one before?" D asks beside me, motioning toward the movie that's almost half over.

I shake my head. "Nope."

"Do you want me to start it over?"

"It's okay."

"You sure?"

"Yeah," I answer him.

"How will you know what's going on?"

With a pathetic laugh still laced with sadness, I explain, "Because that's the beauty of Hallmark movies. There's not too much to follow. It's just a...feel-good show."

"A feel-good show, huh?" He arches his brow and doesn't look very convinced. "Well then, would you mind explaining the premise to me so I can catch up?"

"Sure." I smile. "The heroine is burned out from her career and wound up in this small town for one reason or another, most likely to help push her career forward in the job that she hates. Anyway, she meets a sexy, small-town guy, who's likely wounded in one way or another, and he's about to show her the true meaning of Christmas." Then I take a big bite and savor the crunch of the lettuce with the tang of the condiments and the savory seasoning from the hamburger. Oh my goodness, this tastes delicious.

"That's it?" he questions, still hooked on the plot while completely ignoring his lukewarm burger that tastes like heaven.

"Yup."

"Well, alright then." He scoots back into his chair and unwraps his dinner. "Let's see if he can teach me the real meaning of Christmas while he's at it, eh?"

I chuckle. "For that, you need to watch *The Muppet Christmas Carol*."

"Is that right?"

"Mmmhmm," I hum before taking another bite. An

amused grin is plastered on his face as he watches me chew. Once I've swallowed the small bite, I take a quick swig of water, then add, "Unless you're willing to fall for a small-town baker or an innocent nanny, but they don't really seem like your type."

"And you know what my type is?" he challenges.

"Easy." I decide with a definitive nod. "I think you like easy."

"Physically or emotionally?"

"Both."

"Hmph," he grunts. But he doesn't bother to argue with me before stealing a fry from the white bag and popping it into his mouth. "I'll keep that in mind."

We both focus on the movie playing in the background and the storyline that's just like all the others. I soak up the familiarity like a dry sponge while glancing over at D every few minutes to find him just as invested in the story as I am. We eat in silence while the big city girl kisses the handsome country boy. The snow falls around them in a picturesque scene that brings a smile to my lips.

"Is that what you want?" he inquires, riveted by my reaction to the sappy kiss.

Confused, I turn to him and ask, "What do you mean?"

"The guy next door and the PG-rated kiss in a small town. Is that what you want?"

"I, uh, I don't really know what I want."

"Is it what you wanted…before?" he presses.

Before.

It's weird. To break down my life into two separate segments. The before. And the after. I look back at the screen. A Golden retriever runs through the snow toward the happy couple and wags its tail when it finds its owner to have found true love during the Christmas season.

"Tell me," D pushes, distracting me from their happily

ever after.

"Call me crazy, but I don't think guys like that would be able to handle my kind of messy after…"—I swallow thickly —"after everything I've been through. Hell, I'd be lucky to find a gigolo who would want a broken girl like me."

"That's bullshit," he calls me out, his voice rising with frustration. "You know that, right?"

I've pissed him off. I'm just not sure how.

"Wait. Are you mad at me?" I ask.

His trimmed fingernails scrape across his chiseled jaw as his eyes turn toward the ceiling. "You know what? Forget it."

Pushing himself up from his recliner, he goes to leave, but I scramble for his wrist. My fingers don't even encompass the whole thing, but it's enough to make him pause. The heat in his gaze licks at my skin as he stares down at my hand. It wouldn't take much for him to get out of my grasp. Hell, a simple twist of his arm would do the trick. But he doesn't move an inch.

"Tell me," I plead. "I didn't mean to upset you."

Dragging his stare from my hand to my face, he shakes his head. "Everyone's a little broken, Blue. Everyone has baggage—some more than others. But when you find the right guy who's worth your time, they won't give a shit about how much luggage they'll have to carry. As long as they get to keep you for their prize."

"And how will I know if he's worth my time, D?"

That same indecision spreads across his face before he shrugs out of my hold. "Get some rest. We'll talk more in the morning."

Then he leaves.

And I'm left alone.

But for the first time since everything happened, I don't crave the silence and peace that comes with it. I dread it.

I just want him.

10

SEI

WHERE IS SHE?

*W*here is she?

Where is she?

The thought plays on a constant loop. Finally, I crack Burlone's email password. My fingers fly across the keyboard as I search for where the hell my little Peach is hiding. Pushing aside my stringy, dark hair, I scroll through email after email.

Apple.

Apple.

Apple.

So many fucking apples. And each of them was a dime a dozen. Ugly women in the wrong place at the wrong time. Ripe for the picking. But my Peach? She was special. And I need to find her. There isn't anything about passion fruit in Burlone's emails. And even though my little Peach technically classifies as a passion fruit with her pretty face and hymen still intact, she's still my little Peach. Delectable. Liked to explode on my tongue as I'd dig my teeth into her. Closing my eyes, I remember how sweet she tasted. Like candy. My mouth waters, and my cock hardens in my slacks.

Where is she?

With a tortured groan, I continue my search.

An email catches my eye. It's dated three days before the tournament. Glancing at the clock, I open the email. Transcripts for a shipment. Requesting a sweet piece of unbruised fruit. Passion. One that had been discussed during a verbal agreement. To be delivered to Harry Johnson. Cocking my head to the side, I stop. The name is familiar.

There's an address. I jot it down on my forearm with a Sharpie before capping the pen.

Seems I have a visit to make.

11

DIECE

"Alright, Q. You ready?" I ask. The fan is blowing cool air down on us in the gym, and she rubs her hands against her bare arms as she bounces on the balls of her feet, trying to get pumped.

"Yeah. I'm ready."

Striding over to the back corner of the room, I begin my search for today's equipment. A cabinet tucked against one of the walls holds a few less conventional pieces of equipment, and I smile when I find exactly what I'm looking for.

"Today, we're gonna practice using—and defending against—knives."

"With *that*?" She eyes the knife in my hand. Her wariness is palpable, but I'm proud she hasn't let her fear control her so far. Not yet, anyway. After her meltdown in the theater, she's been more present and hasn't been getting lost in her past. But the fact that I almost kissed her when she was at her most vulnerable?

So messed up.

"It's a theater prop." I point the sharp side of the blade toward my open palm, then push it down until the spring in the hollow handle eats it up, making it look like the blade is embedded in my skin. "We're going to practice with it."

"You're sure this is a good idea?" Her eyes are glued to the knife.

"Yeah. Positive." Striding over to her, I offer it with an open palm. "Touch it. It can't hurt you."

Her hands are sweaty, and she wipes them against her white tank top before taking it from me. It clatters to the floor. With a deep breath, she squats down and picks it up.

"Sorry," she mumbles. "Butterfingers."

"I'm just glad it was the prop. Could've lost a toe," I joke, trying to put her at ease.

She gives me a tight smile before running the pad of her thumb along the dull blade.

"See?" I prod. "Fake."

"Okay. What do I do with it?"

"Try to stab me."

Eyes widening, she jerks back. "What?"

"It's fake," I reiterate. "I want you to try to stab me with it so I can show you how to counter the move. Then you can try."

"He never tried to stab me."

"Yeah, but he could've, which is why you were paralyzed anytime he threatened you with it. Am I right?"

Her white teeth dig into her lower lip before she concedes, "Good point. So I just…try to stab you?"

"You're cute when you're flustered. Yeah. Just try to stick me with the pointy end."

A ghost of a smile stretches across her face before disappearing. "Okay, Jon Snow."

"You liked the *Game of Thrones* reference?"

"I may have dabbled in the series. But only the books," she clarifies.

"You read *Game of Thrones*?"

"Maybe."

My cock hardens as my mind conjures an image of her reading––naked––in my bed.

Then she lunges, and the picture evaporates into thin air. I grab her wrist and use a pressure point while twisting her arm at the same time. The prop clatters to the ground almost instantly.

Shocked, she murmurs, "How did you—?"

"I'll show you. Props for striking while I was distracted, by the way," I add with a smirk. Then, in slow motion, I perform the same movement and make her try it on me. It takes over a dozen tries before she finally gets the hang of it. But when she does, her face lights up like the Fourth of July.

"I did it," she pants with a look of triumph.

"You did it, Blue." My chest swells with pride. "How else would he try to use the knife to threaten you?"

She bites the inside of her cheek but doesn't get lost in her past as she answers, "Against my throat."

"Behind you or in front of you? And while you were laying down or standing?"

Dropping her chin to her chest, she reveals, "All of the above."

"Then let's get started."

The next few hours go by in a blur of Jiu-Jitsu, self-defense, and repetition until she's comfortable with a blade pressed to her throat. And the best part is that she hasn't used her safe word. She's getting stronger.

"You're doing well," I praise her with my ass on the ground a few feet away from her.

Lying on her back, she tucks her hands behind her head and looks up at the ceiling. "Thanks."

"What else do you want to work on?"

Her eyes snap to mine, but I can see the indecision in her gaze.

Sensing her hesitation, I press, "What do you want, Q?"

"I want you to teach me what to do if he...if he gets me on my back."

The last time we were here, she lost her shit. I don't want that to happen again. But she's right. We haven't tackled the one position that terrifies her most. The one we haven't faced since the day she used her safe word. And I'm just as scared as she is to hold her down, straddle her thighs, and teach her how to get out of it.

"You sure you're ready?"

She scoffs. "I'll never be ready, D. But it's like you said...I can't let him win, right?"

"Right." Rubbing my palm down my face, I kneel down and crawl over to her. She's in a pair of running shorts, but they've ridden up a few inches since she's on her back. My brows furrow when I notice the angry red marks slashed across her upper thighs.

"What are—?"

"They're nothing." Her knees snap together before she stretches her legs against the ground, cutting off my view.

"Q...." My voice trails off. I don't know what the hell I should say.

Her tone is hushed and indifferent as she answers, "I told you he liked knives, remember? Now let's get this over with."

The weight of the world feels like it's on my shoulders as I straddle her legs. But she doesn't need my pity right now. She needs my strength. And I'm going to give it to her.

"What's your safe word?" I demand.

"I know what it is. Just get to the point, D," she huffs. Her anxiety is making her testy from her current position, so I don't let it bother me.

Jaw tight, I weave my fingers into her short, silvery-blue hair but keep my grip loose. "Your instinct is to get away when you're in this position. To wiggle backward, right?"

She nods and tries to do exactly that, but it's pointless. I just need to tighten my grip, and she'll be screwed.

"What you want to do is the opposite," I explain, keeping my tone even. "Grab my hand that's holding your hair and lock it in place so that I can't move it." Her little hands wrap around my arm, and she hugs it to her chest.

"Good," I praise her. "Now, you're going to use your foot on the same side that my hand is grabbing you and weave it over my leg." Again, she follows my orders, and my chest swells with pride.

"Perfect. Now, you're going to thrust your hips and push up toward the side that we're locked together. I won't be able to counter your movement with my foot to keep my balance, and I'll end up rolling until you're on top of me, gaining the upper hand."

"The upper hand?"

"Yeah. Being on top allows you more freedom and control."

Her mouth quirks. "Is that right?"

I laugh, grateful for some comic relief in this messed-up situation. "Uh-huh. Now thrust your hips, baby. Let's see what you can do."

In slow motion, she pushes her hips into a bridge, and we both roll. Her elated breath brushes against my face before a ghost of a smile spreads across her face when she realizes she's on top of me and isn't in quite as vulnerable of a situation anymore.

"Again," she pleads. "Show me again."

We go over the movement more times than I can count before her confidence starts to shine through her insecurities.

"I think I'm getting it," she tells me as she catches her breath.

"You're doing great, Blue."

Her smile disappears as she gets lost in her thoughts. Rolling onto her side, she pushes herself up and kneels next to me. When a wisp of hair tickles her cheek, she tucks it behind her ear then sucks her lips into her mouth. Even though I can see the question on the tip of her tongue, she stays quiet.

"What are you thinking about?" I prod.

"What if...what if he's still holding the knife when he's straddling me?" she blurts out. "What do I do then?"

Examining the question, I come to a conclusion that I doubt she'll find comfort in, but tell her the truth, none-theless. "With your back to the ground and a knife against your throat, your chances are slim at best." Her confidence vanishes almost instantly, but I press forward. "My sugges-tion would be to figure out how to get him to put his knife down. Whether you seduce him or pretend to pass out so that it's useless for him to keep a knife at your throat...*some-thing*. I dunno. But your best bet is to get the knife away from him so you can flip him over the way we've practiced without worrying about him retaliating."

A fresh wave of determination spreads across her features as she releases a shaky exhale and nods. "Okay. Okay, I can try to do that."

"I know you can."

"And, uh...what if he's *between* my legs? Not just strad-dling me. What then? How do I counter it? How do I get him off me?"

Squeezing my neck, I drop my head back and stare up at the ceiling. I can't do this. I can't get between her fucking thighs. I can't put myself in that position. Not when I've wanted her since the moment we met in Kingston's office. Not when she's been abused. Not when she doesn't want me the way I want her.

I can't.

"D," she whispers before reaching out and touching my knee.

"I think we've had enough training for one day," I bite out.

"I need to know. I need you to teach me. Please?"

Tortured, I look down at her. "Q—"

"Please?" she begs. "I need this. I need to know I have control over the situations that have been haunting me, and you're the only one I trust. Please? For me?"

Trust. And what if she feels my fucking erection against her? Will she still trust me then?

"Come on, D. I need you."

"It's not that easy," I hedge.

"What do you mean?"

My frustration spikes, and I push myself to my feet then look down at her on her knees. In front of me. With those big doe eyes looking up at me with an innocence she can't fake.

I'm going to hell.

"Talk to me," she pleads.

Now she's begging? Does she want me to have blue balls for the rest of the week?

"You wanna talk?"

"Yes," she whispers.

"Fine. I'm attracted to you," I growl. "I want you to *want* me between those thighs, Blue. I want to erase every single touch he ever laid on you and replace it with my own. I want to show you what sex should be like instead of the nightmare you experienced over and over again at the hands of that bastard who hurt you. And now you're asking me to slip between your thighs." I laugh, but there isn't any humor in it. "I wish I had that much control, Q. I really do. But I can't guarantee that I won't get a hard-on right now, especially when you look at me like that. Like I hung the fucking moon."

79

"Diece—"

"No. If I ever get between those thighs, it's because you asked me to be there. And that's not today. So you'll have to excuse me while I go take a breather and a cold shower."

Then I leave, and I don't turn around to see her reaction. Because if there's any lust there, I'll be a goner. She's not ready for that.

And if there's only disgust? I'll be wrecked.

12

SEI

Clicking my tongue against the roof of my mouth, I light another cigarette. The smoke fills my lungs and calms my nerves as I find the motherfucker at Johnson's house. What the hell is Dex doing here? And with one of Kingston's men? Do my eyes deceive me?

Little turncoat. I smirk.

Once I find my Peach, I'll deal with him and his betrayal. But for now, I have my eyes on my prize. My car is parked a few houses down. But I can still see it all. They're not very discreet. The white sheet is stained. But I guess it does the job of covering up the corpse. Still. You'd be a fool not to piece together that the two men in suits are up to no good.

People see what they want to see, though. I don't know why I'm surprised. So for Dex and his little friend here, they're just a couple of suave bastards moving a piece of antique furniture.

But I know better.

And I'm pissed they got here first. Now, I can't have a chat with Johnson to see if he knows where my little Peach is. After they pull away from the curb, I check the time on the radio.

I don't have much time before the clean-up crew will get here. With a flick, the cigarette butt soars out the driver's side window. Then I jog inside. The first floor is left untouched, but a spot of blood stains the cream carpet on the stairs. I follow it to the crime scene. They're gonna have a hell of a time cleaning this up. A blood splotch the size of a basketball is at the foot of the bed in the master suite. Interesting. When I spot a laptop on a dark table, I grin. Then I step around the mess and sit in the office chair. Johnson's computer is password protected. Figures. I glance over my shoulder and inspect the murder scene one more time.

The clean-up crew will be here any minute. I don't have much time.

Fucking passwords.

Pinching the bridge of my nose, I take a few stabs in the dark. But a bloodcurdling scream makes me pause. I turn around and find the culprit. With a wicked grin, I take in the little boy. His backpack falls at his feet as his wide eyes look like they're seconds from popping out of his head.

"Hello," I greet him. "Perfect timing. Is your mother home too? Or is it just you?"

His feet stay planted in the same place for a split second. Then he's racing down the stairs as fast as his little legs can carry him.

The chase is on.

My laughter echoes throughout the eerily silent house as I latch on to his shoulder at the bottom of the steps. Dragging him back up the stairs, those same little legs kick at nothing but air. He's a feisty little fella. I shove him toward the computer.

"What's the password?" I demand.

"W-what?" the little bastard squeaks. The scent of piss accompanies his confusion.

Annoyed, I lift my chin toward the computer and repeat, "What's the password?"

"I-I don't know it."

I pull the knife from my pocket and let the light glint off the sharp blade. "Better think of something, little boy. I'd hate to have to persuade you."

"P-please—" he starts.

My lips stretch into a wide grin. He snaps his mouth shut.

Waving my hand through the air, I quip, "Please. Continue. I love to hear people beg."

The sound of an engine rumbles down the street and cuts our conversation short. I cock my head to the side then add, "But not right now. Make a sound, and I cut your tongue out. Understood?"

He nods.

"Good boy."

Tucking the laptop under my arm, I drag Johnson Junior by the arm. Then we sneak out the back and jump in my car that's still parked a few houses down.

I glance over at the kid in my passenger seat. He looks like he's seen a fucking ghost. My grip tightens around the steering wheel before another lit cigarette hangs from my lips.

Well, that was unexpected.

13

Q

We haven't talked. And I'm too much of a coward to face him after his declaration downstairs. I don't know what to say. I don't know what to do. I don't know what to think, or feel, or…anything. Chewing on my thumbnail, I pace the floor for a few minutes when the sound of Diece's heavy footsteps echo through the door. Only a sliver of light confirms it's still open. But it's progress. Carefully, I press my ear to the door and listen for any clues I might find. After a few seconds, the steps recede, and I'm left with more silence.

Resting my forehead against the door, I count to ten, then open it. A tray with chicken, vegetables, and garlic mashed potatoes sits on the floor. Which means he doesn't want to see me.

My eyes water as I stare at the not-so-subtle sign that I'm not wanted before picking it up and setting it on the night-stand. The damn thing taunts me like a freaking matador until my blood is boiling with rage and confusion.

What am I supposed to do?

Eat it? Let him have sex with me? Pretend he didn't say anything downstairs? And what the hell do I want? I just...I don't know anymore.

An hour later, I put the untouched tray back into the hallway, then leave the door open a crack and climb into bed.

Maybe tomorrow will be better. Maybe tomorrow I'll be strong enough to face my feelings and the guy who's managed to creep under my skin.

Or maybe I'll still be a coward.

～

"DON'T TOUCH ME," I BEG. MY HAIR KNOTS AT THE BACK OF MY head as I shake it back and forth against the stained mattress. "Please, don't touch me."

"But you taste so sweet, my little Peach," Sei coos before unbuckling his belt. "And now you're going to taste me—"

Bolting upright in bed, my chest heaves, and I try to catch my breath. But the images don't disappear. I can still see it. I can still feel him.

I think I'm going to be sick.

"Shhh...." A pair of hands grab my shoulders before brushing away the messy hair in my face. When D comes into view, my eyelids flutter to disperse the haunting memories.

"Diece!" I cling to him like a lifeline and tuck my face into his neck, breathing in his familiar scent that's starting to feel like...home.

We haven't talked. Yet here he is, comforting me even though I don't deserve it.

"I'm sorry," I whisper.

"Stop apologizing, Q."

"I can't help it." My voice cracks.

"Shh," he repeats. "You have nothing to apologize for."

"That's not true. I'm…I'm scared, D."

"What are you scared of?"

Squeezing my eyes shut, I fist the back of his shirt until my knuckles are white. "I'm scared I'll disappoint you."

His muscles turn rigid beneath my fingertips before the rumble of his deep voice breaks the silence in the pitch-black room. "You don't owe me anything. You know that, right?"

"What do you mean?"

"I didn't tell you that shit in the gym to make you feel guilty enough to let me have sex with you. You know that, right?"

"Of course, I do."

"Do you?" he prods. I can hear the disbelief laced into his question, and it nearly breaks me.

"Yeah," I breathe. "I do."

"Then why do you think you would disappoint me?"

Too much of a coward to look him in the eye, I keep my cheek pressed against his warm chest and admit the truth. "Because I'm curious, D. I'm curious too. About what it could be like between us. But what if I freak out? What if I lose my shit as soon as you touch me? What if…even if I want it… what if that's not enough? What if you can't erase his touch? Hell, even a kiss is terrifying." I laugh, sounding like a lunatic before more word vomit spills out of me. "What if I'll always be lost in my own head? What if I'll never get to share that piece of myself with someone I want? That petrifies me."

"Shhh…." The heat from his hand seeps through my tank top as he rubs my back up and down. Over and over again. The gesture is almost hypnotic and finds a familiar cadence with his steady heartbeat that pulses against my cheek. My breathing evens out as his warm breath tickles the top of my head.

"What are you thinking?" I whisper.

"That you're worth waiting for." He pulls me closer, then rests against the headboard and drops a quick kiss to the crown of my head. "Get some rest, Blue. I'm not going anywhere."

I wait for sleep to pull me under, but it doesn't come. Not unless I can quiet the what-ifs that are badgering me.

"Hey, Diece?"

"Yeah?" he rumbles.

"Will you kiss me?"

"I, uh…," he hesitates. "I don't know if that's a good idea, Blue."

"Why not?"

"Because I need to make sure you understand that you don't owe me anything."

"And what if I already understand that?" I challenge, pushing myself against his chest to face him.

"I'm not a good guy, Q. I'm the big, bad mafia man, remember?"

"I know that."

"Then why would you want me?"

"Because I think you could be *my* big, bad mafia man," I tease. His smile relieves an ounce of the pressure in my chest.

"Would you want that, Q? To own someone like that?"

The thought makes me pause before I lick my lips and admit, "I think I could. Might just depend on *who*. Will you kiss me? Please?"

Inching closer to me, he whispers, "What's your safe word?"

"I know my safe word—"

"Say it."

"D—"

"Answer the question, Blue."

"Fine," I huff. "Six."

"And what happens when you say your safe word?"

"You stop," I tell him for what feels like the thousandth time.

"Good girl." Then he inches closer until his breath fans across my cheek, and I can almost taste him on my tongue. I feel like I'm about to die from anticipation before he brushes his lips against mine. The kiss is soft yet laced with a promise that I can feel in my bones. Cupping the side of my cheek, he tilts my head a little to the left, then runs his tongue along the seam of my lips, daring me to open up to him. When I do, I smile before getting lost in his kiss all over again. The air is electric around us as I inch my thigh over his waist, desperate to get closer to him. With a low growl, his hand slides down to my bare leg before his fingers dig into my flesh, begging me to give in and straddle him the way I want. The way we *both* want. I let my body lead the way, running on pure euphoria before my inner thigh brushes against D's erection.

Then I freeze.

Sensing my hesitation, D squeezes my thigh again, then releases his grasp on my leg and tangles his fingers in my short hair.

With a final kiss against my lips, he breathes, "Get some sleep, Blue."

"You sure?" I whisper. The feel of his hard cock has practically branded itself against my inner thigh. "I can—"

"Stop right there, Blue. You don't owe me anything. You never owe *anyone* anything," he emphasizes. "I'm just lucky enough to have experienced that kiss."

"But—"

He presses a soft peck against my forehead. "Let's get some sleep."

My eyes well with tears, but I don't let them fall as I lay back down on his chest and nuzzle closer.

This time, when I close my eyes, I don't see Sei's hungry stare. I just see darkness. And I relish the respite before burrowing closer to my protector. Because if he's by my side, I just might be able to find peace.

14

Q

My skin is slick with sweat as my feet pound against the treadmill. I would've called it a day thirty minutes ago, but the sight in front of me has been an epic distraction from my tired muscles. Diece's knuckles are taped as he continues to beat the freaking punching bag like it offended him. He ditched the shirt almost an hour ago and has been making my mouth water ever since. If it weren't for my past, I'm pretty sure I would've laid down on the floor and offered myself to him on a silver platter.

Especially after that *kiss*. That mind-blowing, earth-shattering kiss. The one that makes my toes curl by just thinking about it.

Then my self-doubt creeps in. If I *did* have the courage to face my fears and offer myself to him, he'd see the bruises. The cuts. The marks left by my abuser. Most of them have faded, but if he looked close enough, he'd find the freshest ones.

He probably saw them that first day when I needed help unzipping my dress. But maybe not. Maybe he was too busy trying to prove that he isn't like Sei to sneak a peek. Or maybe I'm just trying to keep my head in the sand and pretend that I don't have a visible reminder of my captivity with a monster. Unfortunately, the possibility that the guy I'm definitely crushing on has seen them––or will see them soon if we continue down the path we're on––is bigger than I'd like to admit.

Would they disgust him? Would he pity me? It was so dark last night that I doubt he saw them. And he didn't mention feeling them against his fingertips, so that's always a good sign, but...I might not be so lucky the next time. If he even *wants* a next time.

But maybe it's okay to *not* hide the crap from my past. It's obvious that ignoring it hasn't exactly brought me closure. But facing it and accepting it? I'm not sure if I'm ready for that, either.

We haven't discussed the kiss, and it's driving me crazy. It's like it never even happened. I think he wants me to take the lead because he doesn't want me to feel any pressure, but I'm dying over here. Can't he tell?

Convinced my libido is going to drive me insane if I don't steal back a bit of the power that was stolen from me, I decide to tempt fate and find out whether or not I imagined our connection. If it's strong enough to fight off my demons. If it's strong enough to erase Sei's touch. And if it's strong enough to distract Diece from my scars. Both the physical and the emotional ones.

Pressing the red button on the treadmill, I slip off my tank top and wipe my face with it while swallowing back the anxiety that threatens to consume me. In nothing but a dark blue sports bra and shorts, I walk over to the mat and stretch my arms over my head. If he looks closely, he'll see the long, angry scabs covering my back. And only time will tell if he still finds me attractive after studying them.

Here's your chance, Diece. Please don't let me down.

The familiar rhythm of his punching falters as I bend at the waist and touch my toes. Curious, I sneak a peek at him from between my legs. An upside-down Diece drops his arms to his sides. His eyes are glazed with lust, and the heat nearly burns me up on the spot. No disgust. No concern for the broken girl in front of him. Just an overwhelming need that leaves me breathless instead of disgusted. And it spurs me on. I hide my smile when I stand to my full height and stretch my quads by standing on one foot and hinging at the knee with my opposite leg so that my foot is practically touching my butt before casually looking at him from over my shoulder.

"What?" I ask, feigning innocence when I catch him staring.

That same heated gaze slides down my body before returning to my red face. With an amused smirk, he goes back to punching the stupid bag.

What. The. Hell.

I know he wants me. I can see it. Taste it. *Feel* it. Hell, I almost came just by the look in his eyes. How can he dismiss me so easily? Maybe I just need to…push him a little more.

With a huff, I lay down and swing one leg over the other while keeping my back to the surface, making sure to stretch the tight muscles in my lower back. The sound of his fists hitting the bag ceases a second time, but I don't check to see if he's watching.

When I finish with the other side, I steel my courage.

"Hey, D?" I practically purr.

"Yeah?"

"Will you come help me with something?"

His footsteps echo across the mats before he stands over me. All ripped muscles, sweaty olive skin, and swagger that threatens to leave me a squirming mess on the floor. Wiping his mouth, he tries to hide his amusement behind his hand, but I can still see the mirth in his eyes as he catches me checking him out.

"And how can I be of service?" he offers.

"Will you..."—*I can't believe I'm actually doing this*—"help me stretch my hamstring? I think I might've pulled it."

With a wide grin, he studies me for a few more seconds. "Hamstring, huh?"

"Yup. Wanna help me out?"

I don't know who the hell has possessed my body in the last two minutes, but I'm not about to question it. Not when he's still looking at me like that.

My cheeks flush as he kneels beside me. "How can I help?"

I raise my left leg into the air while my back and right leg stay firmly pressed to the mat. "Can you push my leg toward the ground by my head? It'll help me get that deep stretch that I'm looking for."

"Deep stretch, huh?" he repeats with a crooked smirk. "Is that all you're looking for?"

The challenge laced with innuendo makes me squirm before I tear my gaze away from his and stare up at the ceiling.

"Yup," I squeak.

"If you insist."

With his knees planted on the ground near my butt, his warm hands engulf my left calf that's raised in the air. Then he leans closer and puts his weight into the stretch until his chest brushes against the backside of my leg. As my foot inches closer to my head, Diece's crotch inches closer to my center. I can feel his heat. His lust. His restraint. All of it. As he opens me wide and pushes me into the ground.

"Shit, Blue. How far can you go?" D growls, practically lying on top of me. The deep grit from his voice acts like a beacon, keeping me in the present before I have a chance to get lost in my past.

With a tight smile, I answer, "Yoga and running. My two drugs of choice."

When the toe of my shoe finally hits the ground, we're lined up perfectly. His mouth hovers an inch from mine before his gaze drops down to my mouth. But he doesn't close the distance.

"Hey, D?" I whisper.

"Yeah?"

"I liked that kiss last night."

"I was wondering if we were gonna discuss the elephant in the room, or if you were just gonna keep eye-fucking me all afternoon," he quips. "Was this your subtle way of bringing it up?"

"Mmmhmm," I hum. The sound goes straight to his groin. Hips flexing into me, he groans then pulls away as if to rein in his own instincts that are begging to be let loose. The past threatens to close in from the friction, but I push it away and focus on the present. The caramel swirls in his eyes. The dark lashes that frame them. The laugh lines that crinkle in the corners. It's Diece.

"And what are your thoughts on doing it again sometime?" he prods.

I grin up at him. "I, uh, I think that's a great idea."

"Like...right now? Or...?"

"Will you shut up and kiss me?" I demand.

He leans closer then stops before ripping his gaze away from my lips to pin me with his stare. "What's your safe word?"

"Just freaking kiss me, D."

Like a rubber band snapping, he crashes his mouth against mine. The heat from his kiss is scorching, burning me up from the outside in before I tangle my fingers in his short, dark hair and lick the seam of his lips. It's nothing like the kiss from last night. It's...*more*. It's not just physical. It's personal. It's everything.

He opens his mouth wide then sucks on my tongue, pulling a whimper from me as a pressure begins to build in my core. Desperate, I search for the friction that will put me out of my misery while shoving aside my crippling fear.

With open-mouthed kisses against my throat and jaw, his gritty voice only fans the flames as he murmurs against my heated skin. "Do you trust me, Q?"

I gulp and close my eyes, lost in his touch. "Yes."

"Trust me to make you feel good?"

Squirming beneath him with my leg still pressed between us, I breathe, "Yes."

He sucks the sensitive patch of skin beneath my ear. "Good girl."

I have no idea what I just agreed to, but I'm too lost in this moment to ask for clarification.

With his hand pressed to my upper thigh, he slides down my body before hooking my leg on his shoulder and running his nose along the seam of my crotch.

Oh. That's *what I agreed to. Umm....*

Breathing deep, he groans. "Shit, Blue. You smell incredible."

A blush spreads across my face as I bite my lip and peek down at him. Between my thighs. My thighs that are spread apart like a freaking buffet. His dark eyes meet mine before he hooks his fingers into the waistband of my shorts. But he doesn't pull them down. No, he wants permission. Again. Because this isn't about him. It's about me. My heart pounds beneath my ribcage as I let my leg that was propped on his shoulder drop to the ground. With my soft nod, he tugs my shorts down my legs. Inch after inch. Until I'm left bare.

Which is both terrifying and exhilarating at the same time.

My anxiety spikes as I wait for the moment he'll find more of the angry, red scars that dance along my inner thighs. Because this is the moment I've been dreading. The moment where I'll find out if I'm still beautiful or if I'll always be the broken girl who was abused.

Flinging my shorts over his shoulder, he sprinkles open-mouthed kisses along my calves, inching up to my knees before reaching my inner thighs. Then he stops. Like a caress, I can feel him take in the evidence from my past. With my breath held hostage, I wait.

Please don't ruin this moment, I silently beg. *Please still want me.*

His muscles are rigid, and his eyes darken for a split second, transforming from warm milk chocolate to freaking obsidian.

Shit.

Still frozen, still holding my breath, and still waiting to see his next move, I study him carefully while trying to refrain from building the barrier around my heart any higher. But it's hard to be vulnerable with someone. And I feel *so* damn vulnerable. Especially when the truth is so simple. The ball is a hundred percent in his court.

Then he looks up at me again and holds my gaze while delivering a kiss to each and every one of my scars as if he could take away the pain that accompanied them. His tongue traces the last one before he finally reaches his destination. Separating my folds with his thumbs, he dives right in like a starving man. I arch my back and dig my fingers into his hair, holding him in place as I rub myself against his mouth while chanting obscenities under my breath. The crescendo builds until my incoherent mumbling turns into a loud moan that makes me blush. Sucking me into his mouth, he pushes me over the edge.

My entire body is a trembling mess before my muscles melt into the blue mat beneath me. As I catch my breath, he crawls over me, then slips his tongue into my mouth and delivers a final, toe-curling kiss that leaves me panting for more.

"D," I whisper, reaching for the waistline of his basketball shorts. He gently pushes my hand away and presses another kiss to my sweaty forehead. This one is softer. Sweeter.

"I think that's enough for one day."

"But--"

"Let's get you showered. Then I'll order some food, and we can watch another movie."

He pushes himself to his feet and gives me the perfect view of his very apparent, very hard erection through the thin material of his shorts. My eyes widen as I take in the massive size that could tear me in two.

There's no way that's going to fit.

With a smirk, he offers his hand to help me up and mutters, "It's not polite to stare."

"I can help--"

"I know you can. But today was about you. Come on."

As I lace my fingers through his, it finally hits me. Intimacy is more than sex and getting off. It doesn't have to be selfish. It's about the connection you build with someone. And I'm terrified with how quickly he's managed to form one with me.

15

DIECE

With my arm around her shoulders, and our bellies full of Mexican food, I look down at an amused Q as she watches a Golden retriever devour a wedding cake on the screen.

"Anne-Marie is gonna be pissed when she catches him," Q announces when she feels me watching her.

"Yeah. What's she gonna take to the mayor's wedding? If she shows up empty-handed, she'll lose the big gala event and won't have enough money to pay for her father's surgery."

She grins up at me. "Exactly. Ya know, you're kinda cute when you get invested in Hallmark movies."

"I don't give a shit about the movie, Blue, but I do like to see you smile."

"That seems to be happening a lot when I'm around you."

Pulling her closer, I drag my finger along her bare arm. "We gonna talk about those cuts?"

Like a clam, she closes up instantly and turns back to the movie on the screen, though I doubt she sees a damn thing.

"Not much to talk about," she deflects.

"Bullshit. Did he give you those?"

Scoffing, she counters, "You think someone else would?"

"You want me to kill him for you?"

Peeking up at me, she bites the inside of her cheek. "He's gone, remember?"

"I have my ways," I explain vaguely. And I'd give anything to kill him myself for the shit he put her through.

"I just want to forget all of it. Can you help me do that?"

My phone buzzes in my pocket, interrupting our conversation as I pull it out. Recognizing the number, I grimace then unfold myself from the small couch. "I gotta take this."

"Okay." She watches me for a second, then forces herself to turn back to the screen.

Stepping out of the room, I linger in the doorway before sliding my thumb across the screen to answer the call. "Hello?"

"Hey, D. It's Lou. We have you on speakerphone," Lou explains in a crisp, clear voice.

"Hey, guys," I return. "Who's all there?"

"Kingston, Stefan, Dex, and me," Lou explains.

"Okay. What's up?"

Clearing his throat, Kingston answers, "How's Q?"

I hesitate and glance back into the theater to find Q popping a kernel of popcorn into her mouth. "She's uh...she's fine."

"Has she mentioned anything about her past?" Kingston prods through the speaker.

Rubbing my hand across my face, a little piece of me hates that I answered this call in the first place. Because when I'm with Q, I almost forget the clusterfuck going on at home, along with her part in it all. After clearing my throat, I mutter, "No. Why?"

"Because we had a visitor asking about her," Kingston divulges. "Do you think she's capable of hiding something?"

My jaw tightens until I'm pretty sure I cracked a molar while praying I heard him wrong.

Who the hell would be looking for her? And why would she need to hide something?

Glancing over at her again, my chest tightens before I rub my hand over my face and focus on the phone call. "I dunno, Kingston. I think she's pretty messed up after everything that happened."

"I need you to bring her back here. We need to chat."

"I don't think that's a good idea."

"And I don't give a shit," Kingston counters. "Someone contacted Dominic Castello and asked him to reach out to Dex to see where the pretty blonde virgin ended up."

"Why the hell would someone be asking about Q?" I growl.

"That's what we want to know."

Searching through all the possibilities of who the hell would care about an innocent girl like Q, I ask, "Do you think the guy who contacted Dex might be...?"

"Do I think he might be the same guy trying to screw over the Romanos?" Kingston finishes for me. "I don't know. They might be related. They might not be."

"It's possible," another voice interjects. I think it belongs to Dex, my half-brother. "Dominic said the guy was willing to give me the Romano family as a gift for my loyalty. Sounded to me like he was willing to kill two birds with one stone, ya know what I mean?"

Silence ensues before Kingston grits out, "D, do we know any enemies in The District? Lou tracked Dominic's conversation with whoever his contact is. It led us there."

"But that's Fed territory," I argue.

"It is...," Kingston confirms.

Pinching the bridge of my nose, a single name comes to mind. Jack. He's the guy Acc introduced to us. He helped us frame Burlone the night of the tournament. It feels like a lifetime ago. But it doesn't make any sense.

"We only know one Fed," I mutter.

"Yeah," Kingston breathes.

"Why would Jack double-cross us?" I ask. "Why would he be looking for Q in the first place?"

"I don't know," Kingston answers, his voice crackling through my cell. "But I also don't know who else would be interested in the Romanos or any of the girls who were initially taken by Burlone who happen to work in The District. Do you?"

"Shit," I curse under my breath.

"Who's Jack?" Dex interrupts. He was still Burlone's man when we met the Fed. It makes sense that he hasn't been caught up yet.

Kingston explains, "Jack is the Fed who gave us the fabricated documents that framed Burlone as a snitch. He's also the guy you contacted with the location of Burlone's body."

"So, he double-crossed us?" Dex asks.

"Either that or he works with someone who is double-crossing him," Stefan chimes in with his two cents.

"Regardless," Kingston states, "I think it's time we bring him in for a little chat."

"And if he doesn't feel like talking?" Dex argues.

I can almost see Kingston's arrogant smirk that I have no doubt is stretched across his face. I chuckle darkly before Kingston divulges, "That won't be a problem. Bring him in, Dex. Lou will get you his address. And, D?"

"Yeah?" I answer.

"I wasn't kidding about having a little chat with Q too. Understand?"

Rocking back on my heels, I check on Q again, but she's

too immersed in the movie to sense my wariness. I'm grateful for it. Because she's about to get thrown back into our shitty reality. And it won't be pretty.

Resigned, I pinch the bridge of my nose. "We'll be there as soon as we can."

16

Q

"**Y**ou okay?" Diece asks beside me before reaching over and squeezing my thigh.

We've been on the road for hours, but it's done nothing to relieve the pressure in my chest.

With my gaze transfixed on the passing landscape of greens and blues, I continue chewing on my thumbnail.

"Blue?" D prods.

"I'm fine."

"Liar," he jests. "What's wrong?"

Resting my head against the cool glass of the passenger window, I admit the truth that's been weighing on me since last night. "I don't want to go back."

"To Kingston's estate?"

"To reality in general."

"Why?"

"Because reality sucks. I liked getting lost in my own little world with you."

"So did I." He squeezes my knee one more time before returning his hand to the steering wheel. "Can I ask you something?"

"What?"

"Someone has been asking about you…." His voice trails off, but I'm able to fill in the blank just fine.

A flock of rabid bats claws at my insides, but I keep my chin high and my voice clear as I ask, "Oh?"

"Yeah."

"Who?"

"We're not sure," he returns vaguely. "But we think they're connected with the FBI."

What?

My jaw drops. "I'm not a Fed, D. I swear on my life, I'm not—"

"I know," he interrupts before glancing over at me. And even though his dark eyes are covered with sunglasses, I can still feel the sincerity in his gaze before he reiterates, "I know you're not working with the Feds. But do you know anyone who *would* be looking for you?"

"No one's looking for me," I repeat, twisting my hands in my lap like a dirty dishrag. "We've had this conversation before. I don't know anything. I swear it."

His attention drops down to my fidgeting hands, but he doesn't comment on them.

"Okay, Q. I trust you."

I swallow thickly, then rest my head against the passenger window as my guilt joins the nasty bats of anxiety that are still *very* present inside my stomach. The silence in the cab of the car is only broken by the occasional rev of the engine, but I don't bother to change it. I don't know what else to say, and sometimes it's best to keep your mouth shut, anyway. Besides, when you're locked in a room for weeks, with the devil as your only visitor, you begin to embrace the silence. But today feels different. And I hate it.

"We're here," he announces a little while later as we turn down a long, winding driveway.

I've only been here once before. It was the night Dex drove Regina and me here after the tournament. After I corroborated their lie. After I put a target on my back. One that was even bigger than before.

It feels like a lifetime ago.

"Come on," Diece urges once the ignition is off.

With his hand on my lower back, he guides me toward the entrance. As he opens the front door, a woman's scream echoes throughout the main floor and completely takes me off guard. Crippled by the sound, my knees buckle, and I cover my ears as the memories hit me at full force.

"Stop! Please! Don't touch me! Please don't do this!"

"Shit," Diece mumbles under his breath, barely catching me before my knees hit the ground. His grasp is firm around my waist before he sticks his arm beneath my thighs then carries me to the second floor, taking the stairs two at a time.

But the screams don't stop. No. They *never* stop. The door slams hard against the wall as he shoves it open before stalking toward the bed.

With me in his lap, he rocks me back and forth.

Back and forth.

Desperate to bring me back to the present.

"Shhh," he coos. "Shhh, it's okay."

"Six," I beg. "Six."

"I can't, baby. I can't make it stop."

"Please? Please make it go away."

Laying me on the mattress, he cups my cheeks and forces me to look at him. The warmth in his gaze slowly makes my demons retreat back into their cages as he grits out, "I'm right here, Q. I'm right here."

I wipe beneath my nose with the back of my hand. "I can still hear their cries."

"Stay with me. Don't let those memories lock you in your past. Please."

"I don't know how to stop them. I can still feel my voice turning raw from my own screams as he held me down. I can still see him. *Taste* him," I choke out.

He slams his hand against the headboard then presses his forehead to mine, though his jaw stays tight. He's close to losing his shit the same way I've lost mine.

"You're safe now. You're safe *here*," he promises, focusing on the present the way I should be, but I can't.

Because there's just one problem.

"If someone is so safe under this roof, then what's going on downstairs?" I demand. The tears stream freely down my cheeks as I take in his helpless expression while the wails... the wails keep up their assault.

Brows pinched, he admits, "I don't know, yet. I gotta go figure out what the hell is happening. Can you stay here?"

Grappling with his shirt, I hold him in place, "Please. Please don't leave."

"I'm not going anywhere, Blue. I just gotta check on a few things. You're safe here. I promise. If I didn't believe that, I wouldn't let you out of my sight."

"I trust you, but I don't trust anyone else in this house."

"If you trust me, then you know I'd never let anything happen to you."

His eyes shine with determination and honesty. The combination hits way too close to the chest. And even though I hate how vulnerable I sound, I whisper, "Promise?"

"I promise, Blue." With a slow kiss to my forehead, he slips out of my grasp then strides to the door, leaving it open a small crack before disappearing from view.

Then I'm back to the silence.

And I'm not finding comfort in it this time.

17

DIECE

The main floor is silent. Scanning the empty kitchen, my black shoes scuff against the floors before I stalk toward Kingston's office in search of answers. As I raise my fist to pound on the door, it creaks open then Ace appears with red-rimmed eyes.

"What's going on?" I demand.

She shakes her head but doesn't bother to explain as she slips past me. Attempting to rein in my frustration, I push the door the rest of the way open and find Kingston rubbing his hand against his face.

His troubled gaze snaps to mine. "Get in here."

Closing the door behind me, I take a seat across from him, then rest my elbows against my knees and wait.

With a sigh, Kingston starts, "When did you get here?"

"About the time all hell broke loose. What the hell is going on?"

"Dex. He's been messing around with Regina behind my back."

Feeling like I've been sucker-punched, I scratch my jaw and try to come up with a solution. But there isn't one.

"Fuck," I mutter under my breath.

"Yeah. And that's just the beginning of the shitstorm we're in right now."

"What else?" I demand.

"Jack's here."

"Why?"

Scoffing, Kingston explains, "Showed up on our doorstep this morning. Believes his boss set him up to take the fall for working with Burlone. Says his name is Mr. Reed. Ever heard of him?"

I shake my head. "Not off the top of my head, no."

"Lou's doing some recon to see what he can find. But we think he's the one who was asking Dominic about Q, digging for information."

"Why?" I repeat. It doesn't make any sense.

"We don't know yet," Kingston admits with defeat. "But Dominic Castello is in the basement, and we believe he has a connection to Mr. Reed. We interrogated him before the shitstorm with Dex hit, but I might have a few more questions, so I haven't disposed of him yet."

"It doesn't make any sense," I voice aloud. "She's just a normal girl."

"Is she?" Kingston challenges, resting his elbows on the desk and lacing his fingers in front of him.

I shake off my annoyance and change the subject because honestly? I'm not sure who Q is. The only things I'm sure about are my feelings for her and her shitty experience under Burlone's supervision. "What do you need from me?"

"For now, I need you to stand by me and *not* intervene when I use your brother as an example of what happens when a soldier disobeys my order. Do you think you can do that?"

My jaw tightens as my stomach swirls with acid, but I swallow it back and look him square in the eyes.

"Family first," I answer him.

"Always."

"Where is he?"

Cocking his head toward the exit, he reveals, "In the shed. We're waiting for the rest of the family to get here to hold the communal. Then we'll get it done. Go get some rest. We'll talk more after."

"What are you going to do with him?"

His gaze narrows. "What needs to be done."

Well, shit.

Mind spinning, I exit his office without another word, then find myself outside Q's bedroom. I flex my hand at my side before knocking it against the barely-cracked door.

"Blue?" I murmur. "Can I come in?"

She doesn't answer, but I don't expect her to. She's still shaken from the chaos we stumbled upon when we got here. Pushing the door open the rest of the way, I scan the room and find her lying on the mattress. She hasn't moved since I left her there, and it feels like all the progress we'd made at Matteo's estate has evaporated into thin air. I should've never brought her here.

"Hey," I greet her.

Sensing my wariness, she studies me carefully before coming to some kind of conclusion, though I have no idea what the hell it is. Her movements are jerky, but she forces herself to push past my paralysis and approach me.

"What's wrong?" she whispers.

Pinching the bridge of my nose, I reveal, "My brother messed up."

"Brother?"

"Yeah. Dex," I clarify. "We're blood."

Her eyes widen. "Dex? As in...the guy who worked for Burlone before accusing him of working for the Feds?"

I nod.

"What did he do?"

"Touched Kingston's sister," I grit out, my blood boiling. "How could he have been so stupid? I get that he loves her. I get that she loves him. But doesn't he understand the messed-up position he put Kingston in? He should've been patient. He should've waited until Kingston gave him permission."

She chews on her lower lip, weighing the severity of the situation before a single word slips out of her sexy mouth. "Fuck."

With a breath of laughter—even though the situation is far from comical—I breathe, "Yeah."

"What is Kingston going to do? I remember his warning the morning we returned from Burlone's estate. I remember his threat. His promise. If Dex touched his sister, he'd kill him. But would he actually go through with it?" The question tumbles out of her as her entire body vibrates with concern. For my brother.

Half-brother.

The guy I never got to know.

Regret swells in the pit of my stomach as I answer her. "I dunno."

"Is your boss a man of his word?"

My shoulders fall as I meet her worried gaze and admit, "Yeah. He is."

"Can you talk to him? Say something?" she suggests, scrambling for a way to fix this. But it isn't that easy.

"That's not how the family works, Q." Pulling her against me, I wrap my arms around her naive little body, then rest my chin on the top of her head. I need to touch her. To feel her. Because right now, she's the only thing keeping me from getting lost in the chaos.

"Then how does it work?" she demands.

"Dex knew the rules, but he broke them anyway. Without

repercussions, our world would fall into chaos. King can't let that happen."

"Is there another way?" she pleads, damn near breaking my heart with her concern. She's so sweet. So soft. So innocent.

She really does belong in a Hallmark movie.

Shaking off the thought, I reply, "If there is, Kingston will have to find it. It's not my place. And even though I look at Kingston like a brother, I won't go head-to-head on this. It's his call to make. I respect him, and I respect his decisions. He's going to send someone to come find me when the communal starts. For now, let's just...try to get some rest, okay? It was a long drive, and I'm sure you're drained."

"Both emotionally and physically," she admits with a forced smile before tangling our fingers together. Then she leads me to the bed and pushes me onto the mattress before laying against me. Letting her warmth ease the ache in my chest, I pull her closer, then let the world slip away. Because in this room, with her by my side, I just might have the strength to face it all.

18

DIECE

A loud knock on the door rouses me from sleep.

"It's time. Meet us in the shed," Lou yells. Then his footsteps echo down the hall, draping the room in silence.

"I gotta go," I grumble, untangling myself from Q's sleepy body. Her forehead is warm as I press a chaste kiss against it. Mumbling something in her sleep, she rolls onto her side and tucks a pillow into her chest. My mouth twitches in the corner before shaking off the contented haze I always seem to find myself in when Q's around. As I leave the room, I keep the door cracked then head to the shed.

A sea of familiar faces greets me before we all file into the tiny space where a tied up Dex sits front and center.

I haven't seen him since the night of the tournament. It feels like a lifetime ago. Regret pools in my hollow stomach as I watch him wait for his punishment with his head held high. The bastard doesn't look scared. If anything, he looks resigned and ready to accept his fate.

He knew what he was getting into by messing with Regina. I just hope it was worth it. When his gaze lands on me, his shoulders fall, and he hunches further into the metal chair. I can almost taste his defeat. His regret. But it isn't because he touched Regina. It's because his decision cost us the time we could've had to get to know each other.

And now, it's likely gone forever unless Kingston found a loophole that would still manage to keep his men in line while showing mercy to his newest soldier.

The silence is deafening as the entire room waits for Kingston to make his first move. But the bastard isn't doing anything. He's just standing next to the exit with his arms crossed. The pitter-patter of feet makes my ears perk with interest before Regina appears beside him. Her hair is a mess, and she's panting from exertion as Kingston leans closer to her and whispers something in her ear. Cocking my head to the side, I watch their exchange, more confused than ever.

What the hell is she doing here?

He can't be that callous. Can he? Or maybe Q's making me soft. Then again, it could also be the damn Hallmark Channel.

The tears continue to slide down Regina's cheeks as she listens to Kingston before she gives him a jerky nod, then squeezes her eyes shut and shrugs out of his hold.

Ushering her the rest of the way inside the shed, Kingston begins his announcement. "Gentlemen, do you know why I've invited you here?"

He receives a wave of nods in response, but our silence remains.

Satisfied, he continues. "Early this morning, I found evidence that a man I've trusted, one of *our* men, a man whom I welcomed into the family with open arms, disobeyed a direct order. It's a shame," he admits, his tone ringing with resigned disappointment. "This same man proved his loyalty only hours before when he delivered a piece of vital information to me. Something he could've easily kept to himself if he chose to do so.

Hell, he could've even used it against the Romano family to cause more chaos in an already turbulent time." Raising his hands at his sides, he faces his palms toward the ceiling while motioning to the crowd of soldiers. "The combination has put me in quite the predicament, as I'm sure you can all understand."

We all grunt our understanding.

"But before I reach my verdict," he continues, "it's time for you to all show him what we do to Romano men who fail to put the family first."

All eyes are on me, Kingston's right-hand man, as I raise my chin and stalk toward Dex.

It's time.

Fighting off my disappointment in my own flesh and blood, I cock my arm back and deliver a debilitating blow to the left side of Dex's jaw. His head snaps back before he registers the pain and blinks slowly as he comes back down to earth.

"Family first, brother. Always." I step aside for one of my fellow soldiers.

Face contorting, Dex absorbs the second hit with a low grunt before Lou steps forward to take his shot. Blood gushes from Dex's nose as Lou delivers the next hit and states, "Family first."

Again.

And again.

The soldiers take their turns exacting retribution for Dex's mistake.

Another hit.

Then another.

Until Dex's vision is bleary, and his chin rests on his chest, fighting to remain lucid when he's seconds from passing out. His eyes are almost swollen shut from having the shit knocked out of him, and his nose sits crookedly on his face. But he doesn't beg us to stop. My chest swells with pride.

"Dex," Kingston announces when the last fist has connected with Dex's bruised body. "You came here as nothing but a bastard. You were given the opportunity to make a name for yourself that holds respect instead of shame. Do you think you earned it with your actions, despite disobeying a direct order?"

The crowd is silent, but I lean a little closer, anxious for his response. Because if Kingston doesn't believe it to be the truth, he'll be executed. Appearing desperate, Dex searches the crowd before his gaze lands on Regina. Then an odd sense of peace transforms his features, and it's clear he doesn't regret his decision to be with her.

"Answer me, Dex," Kingston orders, demanding his attention, though I know I'm not the only one who notices Dex's response to the princess of the Romano family.

Kingston can be as pissed as he wants for Dex's betrayal, but he can't deny that his feelings for her are real.

Dex coughs and clears his throat but keeps his focus on Regina as he answers, "I should've spoken up when you first gave your orders. I knew I'd never be able to follow them. I'm your man, Boss. I promise to put this family first in every single circumstance, and I will die for my brothers if the day ever calls for it...with one exception."

Kingston steps forward, forcing Dex to look him in the eye. "I gave you an order—"

"But you required the one thing I couldn't give," Dex argues. "Do your worst, Kingston. I would expect nothing less from the Dark King. But know that I'll never regret touching your sister, and if you let me out of this room, the only promise I'll be able to make in regard to her is that I'll stop attempting to keep my distance. She's mine. She always will be. That being said, if you show me mercy, you won't regret it. I'm a Romano, and I won't let you down."

"Knife." Kingston spits the word like it's a curse before Stefan rushes forward with a wicked sharp blade cradled in his hand. After placing the handle into Kingston's palm, he retreats into the crowd.

Then it's just the Dark King and his victim.

Squeezing my eyes shut, I push aside my unease and wait for King to get it over with. But I can't watch.

The seconds tick by in slow motion before Kingston's voice rings throughout the silent room. "Men like you are hard to come by, Dex. And I'm not sure I've finished having you as an ally." My head snaps up to see Kingston circling him as he runs his thumb along the end of the blade to test its sharpness. "For that, I'll let you keep your life, but not without taking something from you first. These hands touched something they weren't meant to touch, so I've decided to give you a daily reminder about what happens when you defy my orders. If you can accept my punishment without making a single sound, I'll let you keep your life... and my sister."

Dex's swollen eyes widen in surprise, but he doesn't say a word. He's still reeling like the rest of us.

"Do we have a deal?" Kingston prods.

Riddled with disbelief, Dex nods before Kingston questions, "Are you right-handed, Dex?"

Again, Dex nods.

Like a snake, Kingston reaches for his left wrist then squeezes it. "Open your fist and spread your fingers."

Dex's jaw stays tight as he does what he's told and waits for the sharp steel to do its damage.

Then Kingston dives right in, slicing the blade along the top knuckle of Dex's left pinkie. With a soft pop, he dislocates the joint, leaving the finger to hang off the side of his hand at an awkward angle.

Dex's face reddens with discomfort, but he doesn't say a word as his gaze stays glued to his prize. Regina.

With a bit more work, Kingston finishes his punishment and tosses the dismembered finger into Dex's lap as the soldiers witness their leader exact his punishment. One that none of us would like to endure.

"Remember what you saw today, gentlemen," Kingston orders in a loud, booming voice. "Family first. Always. Next time someone disobeys an order, they lose their hand. Dismissed."

And thanks to the display we just witnessed, we know he wouldn't hesitate.

As the crowd disperses, I approach King and pat him on the back. "Not bad."

"You think I made myself clear?" He smirks.

"Crystal."

"Good. Take the rest of the day off. Tomorrow, we'll get back to work and figure out our clusterfuck."

"Hey, King?" I call.

He stops his retreat and looks back at me. "Yeah?"

Tilting my head toward Dex, I keep my voice low so only he can hear. "Thanks."

He nods. "Don't mention it."

19

DIECE

The kitchen is brightly lit as I approach the family table where Kingston, Stefan, and Jack are all sitting. With a river of cards in the center, they finish out their hand of Texas Hold Em' while I pull out a chair across from King and watch.

"Hey, D," King mutters before collecting the chips from the center pot. The bastard won with a pair of aces and kings.

"Hey," I return.

"Get some rest?"

"Yeah."

"Good. 'Cause we're gonna have a hell of a day."

He shuffles the cards and deals a fresh hand but includes me this time before shoving a couple of grand's worth of chips in front of me too. His other half, Ace, taught us all the tricks of poker when King was learning how to beat Burlone at his own game. But we ended up liking the easy pace along with being able to shoot the shit with each other. Therefore, the practice sessions stuck around even after everything fell apart.

However, there's a weight in the room this time. As if we're all waiting for the other shoe to drop. I'd been so far removed from everything that I'd almost forgotten the shit-storm we're in.

"Took you long enough," Stefan calls out as Dex trudges down the stairs. "We're in here."

He rounds the corner and finds us in the kitchen. The bastard looks like shit. His face is black and blue from the well-deserved beating in the shed, and his hand is bandaged up from where Kingston executed his punishment. And even though I've seen a lot of messed up shit, I'll never forget the raw look of determination on Dex's face as Kingston sawed off his pinky then tossed it in his lap.

But even after the doc looked him over, he still looks like he could use a few days off. If only we were awarded that luxury.

"What are you guys doing?" he asks as he takes in the poker chips strewn across the table.

"We were waiting for you," I answer him. "Sorry about your face, by the way. I had to make a statement that I stood by Kingston's decision regardless of what it was."

"I figured." He smirks. "And I would've done the same."

"Good." With the toe of my shoe, I push out the kitchen chair on my right. "Take a seat."

Plopping down next to me, he watches the rest of the hand play out before Kingston gathers the cards and shuffles them together. Once he's finished, he gets to the point.

"As you know, Jack has reason to believe his ex-boss was working with Burlone. We don't know to what extent, but I think it'd be beneficial to find out. Unfortunately, he hasn't tried to contact Dominic's cell—yet. But that might have something to do with the fact that he was trying to frame Jack with the burner."

"What if we pretend to be Dominic and tell him we have

information on Q?" Dex offers. "Maybe he set up iMessage or something and can read the messages through a computer too?"

Nostrils flaring, I point out the obvious. "If we mention Q, he'll know we have her and might come after her."

"We don't *know* that," Dex mutters under his breath.

"Then why the hell would he be looking for her if he didn't want her?" I seethe. "After the hell she's been through, she deserves to stay hidden, and we owe that to her."

Trying to placate me, he raises his hands in surrender. "If Dominic's contact is Jack's boss, then he already knows Q doesn't work for the FBI, which means he won't believe that we put her in the ground like Kingston had told every single person at the tournament."

"We need to know why she's so important," Jack interjects.

"Agreed," Dex announces, shifting his gaze back to mine.

Gritting my teeth, I stare darkly back at him. "I've already spoken with her. She doesn't have any answers."

Kingston leans forward and sets the cards aside, making sure he has my full attention. "Maybe I can help jog her memory."

"I already told you that's a terrible idea."

"And I already told you that she doesn't have a choice. And neither do you."

Growing frustrated, I shake my head back and forth, but I'm careful to choose my words wisely. "She's scared, King. She doesn't respond well to men in general. There's no way she'll be able to answer your questions."

"She seems to respond fine to you," Kingston points out.

With a glare, I mirror Kingston's position, resting my elbows on the table while reminding myself of my own self-preservation. You don't question the boss. I know this. But he doesn't get it. "It's a bad idea."

"And I don't give a shit. I need to talk to her, D, and that's an order. I need to find out if she remembers anything out of the ordinary from her disappearance. I need to find out who she really is because her story isn't adding up, and if she wants my protection, she needs to be honest with me."

I want to argue. I want to drag her away to the nearest cave where we can both get lost, and this entire ordeal will be a distant memory. There's just one problem. Q's screwed-up past isn't just affecting her. It's affecting the Romano's entire operation, and I have to remember the family.

Family first. Always.

But what about Q? my conscience whispers inside of me. Because she's starting to feel like someone other than a random girl off the street that I've been tasked with watching over. She feels like *more.*

Every muscle in my body is coiled for a fight, ready to spring into action at any second, daring Kingston to push me over the edge. But he's smarter than that.

Dex, however….

"She's stronger than you think," he interrupts. "We need to get to the bottom of this."

"Then I stay when you interrogate her," I growl, staring Kingston down from across the table. "And you promise not to touch a hair on her head. Understand?"

The air pulses with that same violent testosterone as Kingston debates whether or not he should let me be there when he questions her.

After another moment of consideration, Kingston answers coolly, "Fine. You can sit in on the interrogation, but if you intervene before she has a chance to explain herself, there will be consequences. We clear?"

My jaw tightens before I spit, "Yeah. We're clear."

"Good. Next order of business. Jack, your face is plastered all over the news. Thankfully, they haven't found any connection between you and the Romano family, but you're officially on house arrest until we figure this shit out. I don't need the Feds knocking on our door with an arrest warrant for you. Understand?"

He nods. "Yeah. If I can help while still staying under the radar, I'm your man."

"Good. It seems that Jack's face being headline news is rocking the boat a bit with Burlone's previous associates, so we'll need to smooth things over. Dex, this is where you come in. I don't care what you have to say; I don't care what you have to do; you will not let any of this messed-up situation blow back on us."

"I won't." His voice rings with determination as my gaze drops down to his bandaged hand.

Kingston nods his approval. "We won't be reaching out to Dominic's contact until I speak with Q, but that doesn't mean I'm not keeping it as an option if we need to move forward with it. Stefan, do you know if Lou has located Sei yet?"

My brows furrow as I register his comment, convinced I've heard him wrong.

Located Sei? Why would we need to locate him if he's in prison?

Blood boiling, I shout, "What?"

Again, all eyes turn to me as my chest heaves with rage.

With a sigh, Dex explains, "Dominic informed us that Sei wasn't captured during the raid."

"But I thought you—"

"Yeah, I know," he replies, growing impatient. "I zip-tied him to a fucking chair and shot enough drugs into his veins to take down a gorilla. I have no idea how he escaped, but he did."

I shake my head, seconds from losing my shit in front of everyone as I order, "We need to find him."

"He's not our greatest concern right now," Kingston counters.

"I don't give a shit what our greatest concern is." My chest heaves. "He was obsessed with her, King. You have no idea the shit he put her through."

"I can imagine," Dex interjects. "And if anyone has a beef with the bastard, it's me. We'll take care of him too. I promise. But first, we need answers."

Kingston grits his teeth before finishing, "And we need them now."

Shoving myself away from the table, I pace the kitchen floor while wrestling with my fury.

"D," Kingston orders. "Get Q and meet me in my office. Everyone else is dismissed."

The sound of chairs scraping against the floor echoes around the room before everyone shuffles away, leaving me alone. I breathe deep, searching for a sense of calm, but anytime I close my eyes, I see the scars dancing along Q's skin. The bruises marring her cheek and back. The tears dripping off her chin because it's too much of an effort to wipe them away.

And it's all because of Sei. He's still out there. The bastard that hurt her is walking around. *Free.* The last of my restraint snaps. I pick up a glass from the table and chuck it against the wall. It shatters on contact but does nothing to stop me from unraveling.

I stare at the shattered glass for a few more seconds, then steady my breathing and head toward the stairs in search of Q. She deserves to know that her monster is still out there. I just don't know how to break it to her.

And King's right. If I'm going to be able to protect her, then we need answers.

My legs feel like lead as I trudge down the hallway toward her room. Tapping my knuckles against the cracked door, I wait for her to answer with my chin to my chest. A few seconds later, her trimmed fingernails peek through the small gap of the door before pulling it the rest of the way open. Her hair hangs wet around her shoulders, and she's in a fresh set of clothes.

"Hi," she greets me with pink cheeks as her gaze drops to the ground. Tight, dark jeans cling to her thighs while a sexy as hell white crop top lets her belly button play peek-a-boo. When she catches me staring, she tugs at the hem before I grab her wrist and stop her.

"You look gorgeous," I tell her.

"You think?"

"Yeah." A soft smile etches itself onto my face as she tucks her hair behind her ear and avoids holding my gaze. It's almost enough to erase my conversation with King. But not quite.

"Where'd you get it?" I prod.

"Ace. She uh, she got some more clothes for me."

"That was nice of her."

Tucking her hands into her back pockets, she rocks back on her heels. "Yeah. It's not something I'd normally pick out, but…."

"Do you like them?" I ask, tilting my head to the side.

That same blush spreads down her neck before she peeks up at me and smiles. "Yeah. I think I do."

"Then that's all that matters." Lifting her chin with the pad of my finger, I add, "King wants to talk with you."

"Why?"

"Because we gotta figure out who's looking for you, Q."

Like a bucket of ice water has been dropped over her head, she gasps and rushes out, "No one's looking for me."

"And we believe otherwise." Keeping my tone gentle, I prod, "Are you hiding something, Blue?"

She shakes her head back and forth, avoiding my gaze

again. Only this time, I'm afraid it's for an entirely different reason.

"Tell me," I push.

"There's nothing to tell. I don't know who's looking for me. I'm no one special, D."

"And I beg to differ. Come on. Let's get this over with." With my hand against her lower back, I lead her to Kingston's office. My steps are slow as I search for a way out of this. But there isn't one.

King's right. She's hiding something. I just wish she trusted me enough to tell me what it is without Kingston getting involved.

The door to his office is open as we step inside. With his fingers steepled and his elbows resting against the desk, he taps his lips and inspects Q.

Like a raisin, she shrivels under his scrutiny and leans into my side.

Kingston quirks his brow but doesn't comment on it as he orders, "Take a seat, Q."

Shaking, she sits down on the edge of the cushioned chair across from Kingston then folds her hands in her lap.

"Look at me, Q," Kingston demands, coolly.

Her trimmed fingernails dig into her palms, and her teeth bite into the inside of her cheek before she forces herself to look at him.

"It's time we have a little chat."

Q

I stay silent but hold his gaze and swallow back the bile that creeps up my throat. I am so freaking screwed.

"Who are you?" he demands.

"Queena."

"And what's your last name?"

"K-Kowalski."

Satisfied, Kingston urges, "Do you have any family?"

I shake my head.

"No mother? No father?" Kingston prods.

Again, I shake my head.

"So you just miraculously appeared as a grown adult?" he challenges with a dry laugh. "Who raised you? Are they alive? If not, then how did they die? Do you have any grandparents? Siblings? I'm going to need details if we're going to figure this out."

My knee bounces up and down as I offer him a noncommittal shrug and deflect, "There's nothing to figure out."

"And I disagree. Listen, I want to make this as painless as possible for you."

A low growl escapes D from beside me, cutting Kingston off. "Careful, Boss."

Kingston's intensity snaps to D before he leans back in his chair and raises his brows, practically begging D to confront him. "Something you'd like to add, Diece?"

"She's scared."

"She should be scared. She should be fucking petrified. Half the mob thinks she's a Fed and is hunting for her head right now. Others are sniffing around, asking questions about her, and yet the *one* family offering to protect her seems to be the last to know the truth." Turning to me, Kingston adds, "You need to start talking, Q. You don't have a choice anymore."

"I can't," I whisper. "I can't do this."

Kingston's expression stays calm and indifferent. But the truth stays the same. He's my judge, jury, and executioner.

"Like I said, you have no choice."

Desperate, I turn to Diece and reach for him. "D—"

"Do you want him to lose a hand right now, Q?" Kingston interjects, that same cool indifference oozing from every pore.

"What? No, I—"

"Because if you walk out that door, then that's exactly what's going to happen to him. Now, let me ask you one more time. Who. Are. Your. Parents?" He emphasizes each word by slamming his hand against his desk.

I flinch every single time before steadying my breathing and peeking up at a very pissed off D who's practically vibrating with anger. He looks like he's two seconds from snapping Kingston's neck, and I can't let that happen. Not when he'll lose a freaking hand. Is Kingston serious? Would he really do that? He's a mob boss. Of course, he'd do that. I can't breathe.

Is it hot in here? How do I get out of this?

"Answer the question," Kingston growls.

"Julia and Alek," I choke out. "Both died in a car accident a few years ago. No grandparents or siblings."

He nods his approval. "Do you have any misdemeanors? Felonies? Any run-ins with the law?"

"No," I choke out again. My throat feels like it's closing up as I try to focus on the scary-as-shit guy in front of me.

"What did you do for a living? Where did you work?"

"It doesn't matter—"

"Answer the question."

My knee could rival a jackhammer as my heart practically beats out of my chest. But he doesn't understand. I can't answer this question. I can't.

Cocking his head to the side, Kingston inspects me closer before realizing how close he is to the truth. I can see it in his eyes.

"Now, Q," he orders.

"I was a"—I release a shaky breath—"a nanny."

"A nanny?"

"Y-yes," I stutter.

"And why didn't they file a missing person's report when you didn't show up to work the next day?"

"I don't know," I lie.

"Bullshit, Q. Answer the question."

My lower lip quivers before I pull them into a thin line. He doesn't understand. He'll never understand. No one will.

"Now," he prods.

The tears run down my cheeks as I turn to Diece and find him staring at me with a restrained curiosity that hits like a wrecking ball. He deserves the truth. They both do. But I can't tell him—either of them. If I do, *he'll* find out. He'll find out, and he'll kill me. I know it.

My face contorts with pain as I swallow back a sob and choke out, "Six."

Diece's eyes widen with understanding before he rubs his hand over his face. "Shit," he curses under his breath. Standing to his full height, he towers over Kingston and announces, "That's enough for today."

"Bullshit, D. She's hiding something."

"She's done--"

"And I don't give a shit." That same calm and collected tone filters through the air. "She does not leave this room until she answers my questions."

"No. You've pushed her too far," D argues, pulling me into his arms. Vibrating with anxiety, I cling to him like a lifeline. Like he's my savior. My *everything.*

"And I will keep pushing until she starts talking," Kingston replies. "Now, I order you to sit your ass back in that seat, or I'll make what happened to Dex look like child's play. This is not a game, D. And she is not a child. Stop coddling her."

"You don't understand--"

"I understand perfectly," Kingston counters. His tone softens as he stares back at his best friend. "She's not a job anymore. She means more to you. I get it, okay? But if you want to keep her safe, then you need to convince her that we aren't the enemy. We're her only fucking hope." Then he turns to me and pins me with his stare. "Who are you trying to protect, Q? What aren't you telling us?"

"What did you do to Dex?" I breathe.

"I cut off his pinkie for disobeying a direct order. Now, if you want Diece to keep his hand, I suggest you stop putting him in a position where he needs to choose between his family and you. The ball's in your court."

"What kind of sick monster would do that to his best friend?" I spit.

"One that puts family first." Kingston leans back in his seat as if we're talking about the weather instead of dismemberment and waits to see my next move. Because he's right. The choice is mine. And I can't let him hurt Diece.

"Let's go, Q," he urges.

"No." I squeeze my eyes shut and dig my heels into the ground. "I'll talk. I'll tell you everything."

With his dark flinty gaze on mine, Kingston murmurs, "Good. Sit back down."

Wiggling from Diece's grasp, I fall back into my chair and pull my knees to my chest, then rest my chin on my knees.

Satisfied, Kingston turns his attention back to his right-hand man. "Sit down, D. I just want to talk."

Jaw tight and nostrils flaring, Diece sits beside me.

Then we both wait for Kingston to continue.

"Why didn't the family file a missing person's report?" Kingston repeats.

"Because they knew who'd taken me."

"How did they know?"

My throat feels like the Sahara Desert, but I ignore the discomfort and mumble, "Because they were working with Burlone."

Unconvinced, Kingston clarifies, "You were nannying for a family in the mafia?"

With a dry laugh, I shake my head back and forth. "I didn't know I was doing that. I thought they were just...a regular family. They don't even have an Italian last name or anything. How was I supposed to know what I was stepping into when I accepted the job?" My voice cracks as I fight back the urge to run away and cry. It's too real. Too fresh. Too close to the threat that could kill me if the truth ever slipped free.

But the irony is that I'm not even sure what the truth is. Just that I need to protect it at all costs if I want to keep my life.

A heavy silence follows as the two men in the room let

my comment marinate. Then Kingston continues. "What was the name?"

"J-Johnson," I reveal.

Kingston's eyes flash with recognition before returning to indifference. If I'd blinked, I would've missed it. Clearing his throat, he asks, "Why would Johnson be okay with your disappearance?"

"He wasn't okay with it. He liked me. Probably too much, but he was always respectful."

"What do you mean, probably too much?" D growls beside me.

Pulling my lips into my mouth, I replay all the little signals from what feels like a lifetime ago before giving him a shrug. "I don't know how to explain it. Maybe it's a weird sixth sense or something. But sometimes, a girl can just tell when someone is looking at her in a…more intimate way."

His nostrils flare. "Did he ever touch you?"

"No. Mr. Johnson never touched me."

"But he didn't want Burlone to take you from him," Kingston interrupts.

"N-no," I stutter. "I don't think so."

His fingers are laced in front of him and rest on the top of his desk as Kingston questions, "Then why did Burlone do it? He wasn't known for selling women who were employed by someone in the business. That's not exactly discreet."

"I…." I pull my lips into a thin line, then glance over at Diece. His pained expression nearly cripples me.

Sensing my reservations, Kingston continues with his interrogation. "Tell me about the night you were taken."

"I-I don't know," I lie again.

"Then think."

With my head in my hands, I block them out and try not to pass out from hyperventilating.

I can't tell them. He'll kill me.

D reaches over and rubs my back, bringing me back to the present as his rich voice rolls over me. "You can do this, Q. Talk to me."

"I can't."

He sighs but continues to comfort me with his touch.

"You can trust me, Q. I'll keep you safe. I promise."

It's the plea on his tongue that does me in. The memories of our moments together. The trust that he's managed to gain despite my best efforts to push him away. All of it.

Before I can stop myself, the truth tumbles out of me, gaining momentum as each word rolls off my tongue until I'm not sure I can stop.

"Two men showed up. It was out of the blue. Mr. Johnson had a lot of visitors, but it usually wasn't when I was there. That's just what Will would tell me. I was upstairs putting him to bed when someone started pounding on the front door. Mr. Johnson answered it, then they shoved themselves inside and started talking." My voice trails off, and I cover my ears, praying I could take the memory away.

"What were they talking about, Q?" D murmurs beside me.

"Someone died, and they needed to get rid of the body. A rat in the Romano family had been found, and they couldn't find a new one. The men were too loyal. But they didn't know what the rat said before he was…taken care of. I don't know. It didn't make any sense at the time."

"And you're sure you heard Romano?"

"Like the cheese," I answer with a pathetic laugh. "Yeah. I'm positive."

"Any other names?"

"V-Vince? I think? He was the rat."

"Yeah. We killed him a couple of weeks before you were taken," Kingston confides, like admitting to murder isn't that big of a deal. "What else?"

Still reeling from his confession, I stutter, "I-I don't know."

"Try, baby," D encourages, continuing to rub his massive hand up and down my back. "Think hard. You can do this. Do you know who the men were?"

Brows pinched, I answer, "Burlone was one of them."

"And the other?"

"Mr....Mr. Reef? Reams?" My face scrunches as I scour my memory. "Reed? Yeah, Mr. Reed."

Kingston's gaze darts over to Diece, and a silent conversation passes between them before Kingston keeps his tone gentle and asks, "Then what happened, Q?"

"Then they saw me at the top of the stairs, and Reed lost his mind." I gulp. "Told Mr. Johnson he was supposed to be alone. Mr. Johnson argued that he didn't know they had a meeting that night, and it wasn't his fault." Closing my eyes, I get lost in the memory and admit, "I can still see the barrel of his gun pointed at me."

"Who's gun?" D whispers.

I force myself to open my eyes. "Mr. Reed's. He pulled a gun on me, but Burlone stepped into the line of fire and told him that he had a better idea. One that was more...lucrative," I choke out. "I freaked out and tried to run to the door, but Reed stopped me and hit me with the butt of his gun. Then I blacked out and woke up in Burlone's office. That's it. That's what happened to me."

The room is quiet, but I can feel both of them staring at me. Not like I'm a monster or the enemy. But like I'm an asset. A piece to a puzzle I had no idea existed.

Reaching for me, D tangles his fingers with mine, then tugs me into his lap. "Why were you so terrified to tell us?"

"Because Reed is still out there. If he knows I told you, he'll kill me."

"And do you know who Reed is?" Kingston interjects.

I shake my head. "No. No idea. Do you?"

The door bursts open from behind me, and I jump in surprise before turning to it. One of King's soldiers stands in the entrance with a panicked expression. "Sorry, Boss. But we had a gift dropped off, and I think you need to see it."

Pushing himself up from his chair, Kingston rounds his desk and tells me, "Thanks, Q. You have no idea how insightful your past is." Then he turns to D. "Let's go."

They exit the room in a hurry, leaving me alone in Kingston's office for a few seconds before my curiosity gets the best of me. I follow them, practically running to keep up with their long strides as they step outside. The air is warm but does nothing to melt the ice in my veins as I take in the so-called visitor.

What the hell is going on?

On the driveway, a little boy is curled in a ball, clutching his arm to his chest as his body wracks with sobs. I can't see his face, only a mop of brown hair, but he can't be older than ten or eleven. My heart gallops inside of me as I inch closer. He almost looks...familiar. Tilting my head to the side, I try to place him while a wariness eats at my stomach. Then I dig my heels into the ground when he looks up and meets my gaze.

"Will?" His name is nothing but a whisper as it escapes me.

The blood drains from my face. Then I fall to my knees.

21

DIECE

The kid's brown hair is damp with sweat and clings to his forehead, and his brown eyes are pinched in pain while he holds his arm to his chest and cries.

He's terrified out of his mind. And I have no idea who the hell he is.

Scanning the premises, I search for anything out of place, but everything appears to be normal.

"Lou, are we clear?" I bark.

"Yeah. Not a soul in sight."

"Who is he?" Kingston demands, stalking toward the kid. He cowers like an abused dog at the pound before Kingston stops short and turns to Lou.

"A dark sedan pulled up near the curb down the street," Lou explains. "Then this kid stumbled out the passenger side before it drove off."

"Will?" a feminine voice whispers behind me.

Curious, I glance over my shoulder. Q looks like she's seen a ghost and collapses on the front steps like a rag doll. Rushing toward her, I push the hair out of her face and force her to look at me. "What did you just say?"

"Will," she repeats, her voice cracking. "It's Will."

"Go upstairs, Q," I demand.

Motioning to the kid, she argues, "But he needs my help––"

"No." I shove her inside. "You're not safe out here. Go to your room and wait for me."

"D—"

"I'm serious, Queena. I'll come fill you in as soon as we get him inside and figure out what the hell is going on. Now, go!"

The indecision is clear on her face before she runs up the stairs and disappears inside the house. As soon as she's out of my line of sight, I rush back out to the shitshow on the driveway and tell King, "It's Will. Will Johnson."

His jaw tightens before Kingston lifts his chin and motions to the kid. "Get him inside."

Having sensed the commotion, Regina and Dex appear in the entryway before Dex asks, "What's going on?"

I ignore them and watch Lou step closer to the kid, but he scrambles away on his hands and knees before Lou can reach him. With a quiet gasp, Regina lunges between Lou and Will then forces the soldier to freeze. "Stop it, Lou. You're scaring him."

"Kingston said to bring him inside."

"And what? You were gonna drag him?" she challenges with her hands on her hips. "He's a kid, Lou. Back off."

Nostrils flaring, he retreats but motions to the kid huddled in a ball. "Then you deal with it."

She glares at Lou with pursed lips, then raises her hands into the air and inches closer to the little boy Q used to nanny.

"Hey, bud." She keeps her tone gentle. "You okay?"

The kid shakes his head back and forth over and over again while his chest heaves up and down with sobs.

"Shhh, it's okay. I'm not gonna hurt you." She kneels down beside him and tilts her head to get a closer look at the strange kid on our driveway. His face is red, and his eyes are practically drowning in sorrow as he finds the courage to look up at her.

"Hey," she repeats, her mouth curving up in a soft, reassuring smile. "I'm Regina. Are you hurt?" She drops her chin to his injured arm, and his gaze follows it.

"I-I'm...yeah. I'm hurt."

"It looks like it. Do you think you could let me take a better look at it and maybe help you feel better?"

His wide gaze makes my gut tighten with pity as he searches her face. Coming to some kind of conclusion, he dives into her arms and loses it. Regina freezes for a split second, her mouth open in shock, before returning his embrace with the determination of a mama bear.

"Shhh," she coos, running her hands through his sweaty hair. "It's okay. It's gonna be okay."

"What the hell?" Lou breathes with the same stunned expression as the rest of us.

"Get him inside," Kingston orders a second time before heading to the front door.

I take a seat across from the couch before Regina, Dex, and the kid collapse onto it. Like a little monkey, Will keeps clinging to Regina as if she's his savior. Depending on how this conversation plays out, he might not be too far off.

Cracking his neck, Kingston sits down in the chair to my right while Lou and Stefan hover behind the couch.

"Hey," Regina croons with her arm around Will's shoulder once everyone is situated. "It's okay. You're safe now. Can I see your arm?"

Whimpering, he pulls it away and shows her the inside of his forearm before nuzzling back into her side like she's his damn mama.

Her hand covers her mouth as she stares at the damage with wide eyes while trying not to freak the kid out any more than he already is.

"Fuck," Dex mutters under his breath. An 'X' is carved into his skin and is an exact replica of the one tattooed on Dex's. Lou rushes out of the room without being told and returns with a first-aid kit as the rest of us sit in silence. Grabbing it from him, Dex sets it in his lap and opens the lid. "I'll take care of it."

We all watch as he starts to clean and dress the wound while Regina murmurs to the kid that he's so brave. That he's going to be okay. That she'll take care of him.

The kid flinches but doesn't pull away as Dex douses it with hydrogen peroxide.

"Why would someone do that?" Lou presses as if Will isn't even in the room.

"It was a message," Dex growls. He's practically vibrating with anger while inspecting the wound again. "For me."

Kingston scrapes the scruff along his jaw. "What kind of message?"

"That he knows I'm here."

"Who?" I demand though I'm afraid I already know.

Dex tears his gaze away from the damage and makes my blood run cold. "Sei."

Regina sits motionless as the name slips out of Dex's mouth before she takes a deep breath and encourages the kid to look at her.

"Hey," she whispers. "Is that true? Do you know Sei?"

The kid shakes his head back and forth. "He didn't tell me his name."

"Okay," Regina concedes with a quick glance toward Dex. "Can you tell me what he looked like?"

Lower lip quivering, he confides, "Long, dirty hair. A diamond tattoo on his cheek. Gross teeth. Smoked a lot."

"Yup, that'd be him," Dex announces, looking like he ate something sour. "Can you tell us how you met Sei?"

Will swallows, then pushes himself up to give Regina a few inches of space as if his fear is finally receding. "I came home from school, and he was in my house."

"What was he doing there?"

"He was trying to get into my dad's laptop. I...I think he killed him."

"Him? Your dad?" Kingston prods before his gaze darts over to Dex.

"Yeah," Will returns. "There was blood all over my dad's floor. He asked if I knew the password, but I told him no. I wasn't allowed to mess with my dad's computer."

"Then what happened?" Regina prods.

"Then he got spooked, grabbed the laptop from the desk, and took me"—he swallows—"took me with him."

"And did you help him figure out the password?" Kingston inquires.

He nods. "Yeah. Yeah, we figured it out."

"Then what?"

"Then, he locked me in a room."

"Did he hurt you in any other way?" Dex asks, trying to keep his tone even. But I know what he's asking. And so does everyone else in this room. He wants to know if he tortured Will the same way he tortured Q. My fists clench as I wait for his response.

"N-No. Just my arm," Will mutters with his gaze in his lap.

A collective sigh of relief reverberates throughout the room. Then Kingston continues trying to piece together the mess in front of us. "Do you know what was on that laptop?"

"Not really. Just work stuff. As soon as we figured it out, he locked me up."

There's a grunt of frustration from Kingston before Will adds, "But he wanted me to give you a message."

Knuckles white, Dex finishes wrapping the bandage around his arm. "And what message is that?"

"He wanted to thank you for taking care of…Burlone? I think that was his name. He wanted to thank you for taking care of him after he betrayed him, and that he…"—his brows furrow in concentration—"that he knows where she is? And that he'll be seeing you soon."

Regina blanches but stays quiet as her fear seeps from her pores. She might not know Sei as well as Dex, but it's apparent she's familiar enough with the bastard to take his threat seriously.

And so do I.

"Regina, can you take Will upstairs for me?" Kingston asks.

"I think I'd like to stay and chat if that's okay?" She keeps her voice even in hopes of not freaking out the kid in her arms, but she doesn't hide the silent plea shining through her eyes, begging Kingston to trust her. To let her stay.

Kingston doesn't answer right away. Jaw tight, his attention shifts from one face to the next before finally coming to a conclusion. With a wave of his hand, he mutters, "Fine. Lou, will you take Will upstairs, then grab Jack? He can stay in one of the guest rooms. I'll have someone bring up some food as soon as we're finished here."

"Sounds good. Come on, Will. Let's go." Offering his hand, Will stares at it for a second, then turns to Regina with a fresh wave of fear in his eyes.

"It's okay," she encourages, rubbing his back. "You're safe now. Go get some rest. I'll come check on you in a few."

His courage is shaky at best, but he takes Lou's hand and stands up from the couch before following him up the stairs to his room. Pretty sure that if it were any other day of the week, the ten-year-old wouldn't be caught dead holding hands with a stranger, but he's too terrified to put on a brave face right now, and I don't blame him.

Sei really is a sick bastard.

Head cocked, a patient Kingston listens to their footsteps creep up the stairs before he turns to Dex and Stefan. "There was a laptop?"

"Yeah. The clean-up crew was supposed to pick it up," Stefan answers stiffly.

"Which means Sei slipped in sometime after you both left and the clean-up crew got there. How big was that window?"

"Thirty minutes, maybe?" Dex rolls his shoulders before scrubbing roughly at his face. "I should've just grabbed it."

"We were a little busy carrying a body," Stefan argues.

"No excuse. I should've gone inside."

"You were following standard protocol. The clean-up crew was supposed to grab it."

"Yeah, but—"

"It's no use arguing over the past," Kingston interjects, but it doesn't erase the frustration emanating from his stiff frame.

A set of footsteps ends the conversation as Jack and Lou come into view.

"Jack, thanks for joining us," Kingston greets him as he appears at the base of the steps.

"Thanks for having me," he quips. "To what do I owe the pleasure?"

"We had a visitor."

"Who?"

"A boy named Will Johnson."

"Am I supposed to recognize that name?" Jack returns as he takes a seat on the arm of the couch.

With a one-shouldered shrug, Dex replies, "Probably not. His dad was a potential buyer for one of the girls and had been working with Burlone before I was sent to…take care of it."

"Take care of it?" Jack laughs. "You mean, you killed him."

"I mean, I took a sex trafficker off the streets. When was the last time you did that much?" Dex challenges.

"Stop," Kingston orders before resting his elbows on his knees. Cracking his neck, he continues. "Listen up because I'm about to throw a shit-ton of information at you. Johnson's son was kidnapped by Sei, who helped him break into Johnson's computer before Sei carved an 'X' into his arm. Then he dropped the kid off down the street and ordered him to walk up my driveway and deliver a message to Dex."

"What kind of message?" Jack asks.

"It was a threat that he'd be seeing him soon and that he knows where Regina is. Why the hell isn't he in police custody?"

"Sei wasn't on the premises when we raided Burlone's estate," Jack answers with a glare at Dex. "We searched everywhere for him."

Ignoring his pissy attitude, Kingston adds, "Yeah, well, his appearance is just the tip of the iceberg. A few minutes before the kid showed up, Diece and I had a little chat with Q. She divulged some information that connected your boss to the mob and explains why he's so desperate to find her."

Jack's annoyance transforms to utter shock. "What? How?"

"She witnessed Reed attending a meeting with Burlone and Johnson. When they caught her eavesdropping, Reed wanted to have her killed, but Burlone figured that selling her would be a more lucrative way for her to disappear. She's the key to clearing your name. Unfortunately for you, I can't allow her to testify."

Outraged, Jack jumps to his feet and spits, "What? Why the hell not?"

Shit, I'd be pissed too. His freedom was at the tip of his fingers, but Kingston just slid it out of his grasp.

Ignoring Jack's outburst, Kingston clarifies, "Because I told everyone Burlone was working for the Feds, and while that's true, it seems that he was using them instead of the other way around."

"And that's a problem because...?" Jack lets his voice trail off and waits for Kingston to fill in the blanks.

Instead, I do it for him. "If it looks like Kingston got his facts wrong, it'll taint the Romano name, and we can't have that now, can we?"

"So, what? I'm supposed to take the fall?" Jack sneers, but Kingston doesn't back down.

"It's either you or the entire Romano family along with an innocent girl who was at the wrong place at the wrong time," Kingston returns. "Tell me something, Jack. Does *that* seem very fair to you?"

The guy looks like he's about to crack one of his molars, but he doesn't cower from Kingston's scrutiny. "And what would you suggest I do?"

Kingston's voice is controlled as he replies, "I suggest you let us take care of your little friend."

"By what? Killing him?" He scoffs. "I'm not a dirty cop."

"You know, I love how you *still* think you're better than us, even when I've opened up my home and have offered to help you. Even when I've held up my end of the deal and delivered multiple sex traffickers to your door in a handbasket. We aren't that different, whether or not you'd like to admit it. But the fact of the matter is that sometimes, we have to get our hands dirty, Jack. Your boss has already made contact with another mafia family. Who's to say he won't do it again? He's connected to buying and selling women. He screwed you over. He deserves to be put in the ground."

"I can't do that."

"Why?" Kingston sneers. "You were willing to get your hands dirty once in order to protect innocent women. What makes this so different? When I found out there was a rat in the Romano family, I exterminated him before he could spread his sickness to someone else. I suggest you open up to the possibility that you might have to do the same."

"You're suggesting I kill Reed? Why can't we just turn him in?"

"The legal system will fail," Kingston reminds him. "Especially when there's now a connection to your sole witness and the Romano family. People will think she's lying. And even if you do convince her to get on the stand and confess—which will put a target on her back from inside the legal system, thanks to your boss, as well as anyone that saw her at the tournament—one witness without hard evidence won't be enough to taint a seasoned Fed's name. Especially when there's still hard evidence against you."

"But it wasn't my phone!" Jack argues, his face flush with anger.

"Doesn't matter. He'll get away scot-free. And your head, along with Q's, will be next on the guillotine. You're fucked, Jack. That might not be what you want to hear, but it's the truth. Now, you have two choices. Either help us handle Reed in our own way so that you can taste an ounce of justice, or deal with the fallout when we don't and live with the consequences."

Like a stick of dynamite, Jack explodes with a violent burst of fury. His closed fist punches through the drywall as a scream of frustration ricochets off the walls. Kingston watches him in silence, patiently waiting for him to finish his little temper tantrum before agreeing to the proposition.

Because he will agree.

Of that, I have no doubt.

"Are you finished?" Kingston states while the rest of the room is blanketed with silence.

Rubbing his hand across his face, he growls, "I can't do that. I'm not that kind of guy."

"Sure, you're not. Whatever helps you sleep at night, Jack. But I put Q under the protection of the Romano family, and I won't risk her safety all because you're adamant about keeping your hands clean. You have twenty-four hours to decide."

With a sneer, he storms out of the room before digging his heels into the ground when Kingston calls after him. "And don't leave the fucking premises! Your face is still plastered all over the news. We clear?"

Nostrils flaring, a pissed off Jack grits out, "Crystal."

Then he's gone.

Unperturbed, Kingston continues. "Now, we have a kid upstairs who's seen way too damn much. What the hell are we supposed to do with him?"

"What do you mean?" Regina interjects. I'd almost forgotten she was here. "We aren't going to kill an innocent kid, Kingston. That's not—"

"I wasn't suggesting that," he clarifies with his hands raised in defense. "Come on, Regina. I might be a bastard, but I wouldn't do that shit."

Tossing his arm around her, Dex pulls her into his side to defuse the situation before thinking aloud, "He doesn't have any family. Just him and his dad."

"And the nanny," Kingston quips. "But I don't think she'll be able to help him right now. What are your thoughts, D?"

A headache threatens to spread from the base of my skull before I pinch the bridge of my nose. "She'll kill me for saying this, but she needs to figure out her own shit before she can take on a kid."

Not a chance in Hell could she take care of anyone right now. She can barely take care of herself. She was doing so much better at Matteo's estate. But now, I'm not sure of anything, let alone her mental health.

My attention shifts to the staircase as I half-expect to see my broken Blue watching me from the top of it, shaking like a leaf, but it's empty.

"I orphaned him," Dex mutters, distracting me. "And thanks to Sei, he wears my mark. So what do you think, Little Bird? Any chance you'd be willing to help me keep an eye on him for the time being? He seemed taken with you."

"We can watch him. At least until we figure out our next step," she agrees without thought, but I'm not exactly surprised. The girl has always been a sucker for taking people under her wing.

Nodding, Kingston divulges, "I don't think he'll try to run. He has nowhere else to go, but he's seen too much shit to be trusted. We also don't know how long it'll be before someone reports him missing. I'll have Lou find him a new social, birth certificate, all that shit once we figure out a long-term solution. But for now, keep an eye on him."

Dex looks down at Regina beside him before they both turn to Kingston. "We will."

"Good." Massaging his temples and likely fighting off a massive headache, Kingston moves on to the next bullet point of today's family meeting. "Now, we need to figure out how we're going to catch Sei. Any suggestions?"

"Use me as bait," Dex offers. "He wants a fight. Might as well give it to him."

Kingston shakes his head. "No."

"Why the hell not?"

"Because if he really wanted you, all he'd have to do is

knock on our door. He knows you're here and that you switched sides. You're not the prize he's looking for. And neither is Regina." All eyes turn to me before Kingston finishes, "Q is."

"Are you suggesting we use Q as bait?" I grit out, convinced I've heard him wrong.

"Listen—"

"No. Not a chance in Hell will I let you put her in danger."

"And I don't give a shit what you want," Kingston counters with a dry laugh, but I don't find much humor in the situation. "She won't be safe until Sei is off the streets. You said so yourself. He's obsessed with her."

"But that doesn't mean I'd be willing to let him get within ten fucking miles of her—"

"What would you prefer, D? We just wait for him to strike when we least expect it? Or create a plan and execute it on our terms?"

And even though the truth is glaring at me, I look him in the eye and argue, "He doesn't know where she is."

"We don't know that," a somber Dex interjects. "Sei knows how to track people. It's why he was such an asset to Burlone."

"No." I shake my head back and forth. "No."

"Why don't you ask Q what she thinks about it?" Regina suggests in a quiet voice before resting her head on Dex's shoulder. "You might be surprised by the risk she'd be willing to take if it were to keep Sei away from her."

"But this wouldn't be keeping them separated. This would be me offering her to the wolf on a silver platter."

"Give me a little more credit, D," Kingston mutters as he rolls his eyes. "Have I ever let you down?"

My lips pull into a thin line.

"Have I?" he pushes.

With all eyes on me, I grit out, "What's the plan?"

147

Kingston hesitates before cracking his neck as if he's getting ready for war. "Dex, you know Sei better than anyone. Any suggestions?"

"Let me think about it, and I'll get back to you."

"Alright. Dismissed."

22

Q

My mind reels from the shitshow downstairs. First, my conversation with Kingston and Diece, then a familiar face from the past shows up to mess with me.

Coincidence? I think not.

What the hell is Will doing here? *How* is he here? Where's Mr. Johnson? Does Reed know I'm here? And if he does know, is he coming for me? My breath hitches.

What am I supposed to do now?

Pacing the thickly-carpeted floor, I weave my fingers through my blue hair and tug on the roots, praying the bite of pain will bring an ounce of clarity.

It doesn't work.

Replaying every possible outcome over and over again, I finally give up and collapse on my bed before holding my head in my hands.

And what about D? Did I just deliver a monster to his door? Not Will, obviously. But Reed? If he finds out I told D, he'll kill him. My head won't be the only one on the docket. D's will be too. And I can't let that happen.

A set of footsteps pique my curiosity as I continue to sit in my room, stewing in silence.

"Stay in here," a low voice orders across the hall before retreating back down the stairs.

Head cocked, I wait for any other clues but don't receive any. There's a moment of silence before I tiptoe toward my door and open it a few more inches. The hallway is empty. With a deep breath, I venture into the unknown and raise my fist to tap on the door that's opposite of mine.

Tap. Tap. Tap.

"Hello?" a little voice squeaks.

Chest aching, I push open the door. "Will?"

"Queena?"

His pre-teen body practically tackles me as he darts across the room and wraps his arms around my waist.

"Queena, where have you been? You disappeared. Dad said you quit—"

"I know, Will. I know." Squeezing him tight, I fight back my tears, then slide to the ground and rest my back against the wall. Will follows suit and scoots beside me, leaving less than an inch of space between us.

"What are you doing here, bud?" I whisper as I take in his profile. I've only known him for a year or so, but when you're with someone day in and day out, you start to know them better than yourself. His cheeks aren't as full as they used to be, and the normal rosy color that I've grown accustomed to is absent. It looks like he's aged a few years since the last time I saw him. And I'd do anything to give him back that time.

"I don't...I don't want to talk about it," he chokes out.

His words act like a vice around my heart. "Then we don't have to talk about it. Just know that I'm here for you, okay?"

"Okay."

"You look tired, though," I point out.

He shrugs but doesn't deny it.

"You should get some rest."

With a quick shake of his head, he mutters, "I uh, I don't like to close my eyes."

A sad yet knowing smile graces my lips before I divulge a secret. "Ya know, I get scared sometimes too. But do you wanna know what helps me?"

"What?"

"I think about the good stuff. Sometimes, if you try hard enough, you can replace the bad with the good. You just have to stay strong and not give in to the darkness."

"How do I do that, Queena?" he whispers.

"Think of happy thoughts."

"Like in Peter Pan?" He quirks his brow in disbelief.

"Exactly," I chuckle before bopping him on the nose with my index finger.

"And that really works?"

"Not all the time," I admit. "But it definitely helps."

Peeking up at me, he asks, "What's your happy thought?"

An image of D immediately comes to mind. His eyes are alight with fascination as he pops another kernel of popcorn into his mouth while staring at an über-cheesy Hallmark movie. The plot might as well involve aliens for how foreign it is to a guy like him, but he's as entertained as ever. And I know it's because he wants me to be happy and will do everything in his power to make it happen, even if it involves sitting through a predictable, sappy love story.

"Queena?" Will murmurs, pulling me back to the present.

I toss my arm over his skinny shoulders and tug him into my side. "Get some rest. I'll hang out with you here and keep the monsters away, okay?"

With a loud yawn, he scoots down then rests his head on my lap while his gangly body spreads out across the floor.

There's a king-sized bed a few feet away, but I don't mention it. He looks too exhausted to move anyway.

"Thanks for being here, Queena," he whispers as his heavy lids flutter closed.

"Anytime."

Running my fingers through his brown mop of hair, I think back on how much our worlds have been flipped upside down in such a short amount of time. But there's no use getting lost in the past and what coulda, woulda, shoulda been. Diece taught me that. And now, I'm going to do my best to pass on the knowledge to this kid who, in the blink of an eye, got dealt a pretty shitty hand too.

My head rests against the wall behind me as I fight off the exhaustion that overwhelms every inch of me. I'm crashing. Hard. After the adrenaline rush from earlier, I'm not exactly surprised that I feel like a drained battery, but that doesn't stop me from fighting to keep my eyes open. I'm not sure how much time passes before I realize I've lost the battle. Caught between oblivion and a meditative state of peace, a panicked voice filters in from the hall.

"Q? Q, where are you?" Heavy footsteps stomp around the hallway, searching for me before I register what the hell is going on and whisper-shout, "Diece! Diece, I'm in here."

The pounding ceases. "Q?"

"In here."

Will's door opens seconds later to reveal a disheveled Diece. Pressing my index finger against my lips, I whisper, "Shhh."

His eyes widen as he assesses my position and the boy lying in my lap before he squats next to me. "What are you doing in here?"

"Did you honestly expect me not to check on him?" I counter.

"If I've learned anything from you, it's that you've

managed to exceed my expectations on multiple occasions," he mutters under his breath.

"Liar," I quip with a smile. "I'm a mess."

Amused, he tucks my hair behind my ear. "We're all a mess in our own way, Q. The fact that you can even own up to it says something." He pauses then adds, "Thank you for confiding in me and Kingston today."

"I didn't exactly have a choice," I point out.

"There's always a choice. And if I had to have lost my hand to prove that to you, I would've."

"But that's quite the consequence, don't you think?"

"I didn't say there weren't consequences to our actions," he clarifies with a wry smirk. "It just depends on the price you're willing to pay. How's he doing?"

I look down at the little boy in my lap. "Shaken, but I think he'll be okay."

"He looks exhausted."

"He *is* exhausted," I confirm, taking in Will's boyish features. His eyelashes are so damn long. Lucky little shit. I run my fingers through his brown hair again, then turn to D. "Do you know what happened? Do you know why he's here? Does anyone else know *I'm* here?"

"Let's go chat in the other room."

"I can't leave him—"

"Knock, knock," Regina calls from the doorway. Her heels dig into the ground when she finds us huddled together. "Oh." Dropping her voice to a whisper, she hooks her thumb over her shoulder and mumbles, "I can come back."

"Wait," D orders just as quietly before he turns to me. "What if Regina stays with him? Then you and I can talk in private without the risk of waking him up."

I look down at Will again. He looks so little in my lap. So innocent. So tired. Licking my lips, I answer, "Okay." Then I carefully lift his head up and slip out before Regina replaces me on the floor.

"I'll look after him," she promises. The determination in her eyes soothes my nerves, but I still find myself frozen in place until the heat from Diece's palm brands my lower back.

"Thank you," I breathe. Then Diece guides me back to my room.

As I step over the threshold, he grabs my face and kisses me. It's hard and desperate, filled with so much relief that I almost melt on the floor. When he pulls away, a breath of laughter weaves itself into my voice as I whisper, "What was that for?"

"I just needed to kiss you."

I smile against his lips, then rise onto my tiptoes and press a second kiss to his mouth. This one is softer, gentler, but laced with just as much emotion as the first.

When he pulls away a second time, he presses his forehead against mine and squeezes his eyes shut.

"What's wrong?" I ask, sensing the hurricane in his soul.

"Nothing."

Trying to lighten the mood, I tease, "Liar."

"Sorry."

"Don't apologize." His five o'clock shadow tickles my palm as I cup his cheek. "What's going on?"

As if in pain, he closes his eyes and leans into me. "I just… I wish I could protect you."

"You *do* protect me."

"I mean from your past," he clarifies before opening his eyes. The emotion that swirls in their depths is staggering. The guilt he feels for something he couldn't control. It makes me want to cry, and hug him, and beg him to keep me forever. But this isn't a fairy-tale. And he isn't an average Prince Charming.

"In another life, I'd make us hide away at Matteo's estate forever," he murmurs, reading me like an open book.

"But you're a Romano," I finish for him. "And you'd never be satisfied with that kind of life. I've given you the impression I'm broken. And in a way, I have been. But after seeing Will, I know that I can't *stay* broken. You were right. I can't let myself live in fear. I have to be stronger than that. And I need you to believe in me. To let me prove that I *am* stronger than that."

"You're the strongest person I know," he whispers.

"Not yet. But I will be. Now, tell me what you know about Will."

23

Q

Diece tells me every minute detail about Will and Sei and Burlone and Johnson and freaking *Reed* until my head is spinning. But it's Sei's name that makes my gut clench and my muscles tighten with anxiety and fear. Once he's finished, I feel like a boa constrictor is wrapped around my torso, squeezing the life out of me, but I can't ignore it. That will only make the wound fester.

With my head in my hands, I clarify, "So, he really is out there."

"Yes."

"Lovely."

He laughs.

"He'll be looking for me," I confide, sobering as I look up at D. "He promised to never let me free. That he'd always have me. That he'd always use me. And hurt me. And everything else. In his own sick, twisted way, I think he does love me. But it isn't the right kind of love. It's...."

"Fucked-up, Q. So fucked-up."

Rubbing my hand beneath my nose, I sniff and try to

push aside my fear and the memories that accompany Sei's name. "And you want to use me as bait to catch him?"

"I don't want to," D grits out. The defeat in his voice is crippling as he guides me to the bed before encouraging me to sit on the edge of it. When I do, he joins me and continues. "But I'd rather be the one hunting for the bastard than the sitting duck, waiting to be slaughtered."

Well, when you put it that way....

I feel like my veins have been injected with Mentos and Coke. Like my entire body is fizzing with too much carbonation, and I'm going to explode. Wringing my hands together in my lap, I whisper, "I'm terrified, D."

"I know."

"But I trust you." I peek up at him.

The heat of his gaze isn't scorching. It's more like a warm sip of hot chocolate or the kiss of sunshine in the middle of summer that licks at my cheeks as he inches forward and presses his lips to mine.

I melt into him and open my mouth to let him inside when I feel his tongue tease the seam of my lips. His fingers tangle into my hair, cupping my cheeks with his calloused hands. I smile when the rough yet gentle grip scratches my sensitive skin.

I could love this man. I could fall for him. Hell, I *have* fallen for him. And while that's terrifying, it's also freeing.

The sound of his low groan makes my toes curl before I tangle our tongues together and deepen the kiss. Getting lost in his touch, the soft comforter cradles my back before I realize I'm lying down. On a mattress. With a massive, muscular guy that's twice my size on top of me. It would be easy for him to force me to do something I'm not comfortable with. I wouldn't even be able to put up a fight if he decided to toy with the idea.

But instead of being filled with terror, there's a peace that accompanies my realization. Because even though he could do whatever the hell he wants to me, he wouldn't. Not without my consent.

I know it in my bones. I can feel it in my chest. Hell, it's apparent in every fiber of my being. He might be a big, bad mafia man. But to me, he's Diece. My Diece. My protector. My friend. My *everything*.

And that makes all the difference.

With his strong arms caging me in on both sides of my head, I open my legs in an attempt to cradle his hips. Sensing my intent, Diece ends our kiss and pushes himself into a push-up before he stares down at me. His hesitation is clear as his piercing brown eyes pin me in place.

"Blue…."

"I want to."

Tortured, he squeezes his eyes shut. "You don't have to—"

"I know. I said *want*," I reiterate with a dry laugh. "I want you. I want to give myself to you. I want to be with someone that I *want* to be with. And you're that someone."

"What's your safe word, Q?"

"I know what it—"

"Say the word, Q," he grits out. "I need to hear you say it."

The pain in his eyes hits me harder than a sledgehammer. I'm not the only one who's scared. Who regrets my past even though neither of us had any control over it. And for some reason, it's comforting to know that he might not ever understand what I went through or how much it messed me up. But he *cares*. And he'll do everything in his power to make it better and erase the damage.

Licking my lips, I breathe, "Six."

"And if you feel uncomfortable at all, you say that word. We clear?"

"Yeah." I smile up at him. "We're clear."

His Adam's apple bobs up and down in his throat, but he

doesn't move a muscle. Like he's still debating whether or not he should back out. Weaving my fingers behind his neck, I pull him closer until our chests are pressed together. Then I kiss him, silently begging him to stay with me. To be with me. To *not* let my past divide us any more than it already has. Knuckles white, he grips the sheets by my head before groaning and giving in to the temptation that is literally spread out beneath him.

Then he finally snaps. The punishing grip of his fingers digs into my outer thigh as he hitches it over his fully clothed hip, then grinds into me. His thick erection rubs against my core and pulls a whimper from my lips as he continues torturing me with his mouth. His other hand. His soft groans. All of it. Until I'm drowning in need. When I'm positive I can't take it anymore, he trails open-mouthed kisses against my jaw and neck before pushing himself onto his knees.

Hooking his fingers around the neck of his shirt, he rips it over his head then throws it across the room before standing up to do the same to his pants. My mouth waters as I scan all the delicious olive skin covering muscle after rippling muscle.

With a smirk, he jokes, "Like whatcha see?"

My cheeks catch on fire. "Oh. Sorry."

I drop my gaze to the silky sheets surrounding me, hating how quickly my insecurities always seem to claw to the surface. His footsteps make the floor creak as he closes the distance between us and lifts my chin with his finger.

When our gazes connect, a soft smile tugs at the corner of his mouth. "I was joking."

"Oh." I wave him off. "Yeah. I know that."

"I'm serious, Q. You're allowed to check me out without apologizing." He leans in and presses a quick kiss against my lips. "You're allowed to feel lust without feeling guilty." Grab-

159

bing the hem of my shirt, he pulls it up a few inches to reveal my lower stomach. "You're allowed to let go and like sex." The cold air brushes against my bare skin as he pulls it over my head and tosses it over his shoulder to join his own pile of clothes. "You're allowed to choose your partner." He kisses me again. Only this one is much less innocent and much headier. "And I'm the luckiest bastard in the world because you chose me."

His fingers make short work of the button on my jeans before he tugs them down my thighs and follows the movement with his lips, peppering kisses along every inch of skin. Other than my underwear, I'm bare to him. And it's terrifying. Fighting the urge to cover myself up, my muscles tense before Diece's dark chuckle greets my ears, and he tangles our fingers together.

"You're beautiful, Q. You're fucking breathtaking. Now, let me help you let go." His tongue swirls against the scars along my inner thigh, and he glances up at me as his mouth hovers only a few inches from my core. But he doesn't dive in.

He's waiting for permission.

Again.

With a tight smile, I nod.

Then he grins and uses his fingers to push aside the last, flimsy piece of fabric that separates us. Squeezing my eyes shut, I get lost in the feel of his mouth against the most intimate part of me. The part that no one else has touched. Well, other than the last time, anyway. But it's the part that's his. And only his.

My orgasm hits fast and hard as he pushes a finger inside of me and sucks the bundle of nerves into his mouth before I come crashing into oblivion. As I catch my breath, he nibbles, licks, and kisses the skin along my stomach, then stops at my chest and sucks my left nipple into his mouth while palming my right breast.

Holy shit.

How does he do it? How does he make me feel so freaking good when, in other circumstances, it's pure torture?

I squirm and arch my back, begging him to continue as that same, sweet ache starts to build all over again. I can feel his smile against my skin before he gently bites down and pulls a moan from my lips.

"Shit, Diece."

Another smile, then he sucks a little harder before releasing my nipple with a soft pop. I'm seconds from smacking the guy as he stops at my neck and sucks again. I have no doubt I'll have a purple mark there tomorrow, but I don't even give a crap right now. Not when his hands and mouth are roaming my body. Satisfied, Diece meets my mouth with his own and kisses me while lining himself up at my entrance.

"You ready?" he murmurs.

Hooking my ankles around his waist, I quirk my brow and dare him to back out now. Thankfully, he catches my drift. With another dark chuckle, his right hand pins my waist down to the mattress then he carefully pushes inside of me.

My mouth drops open as my vision blurs until all I can see, smell, and feel is him.

Shiiit that hurts.

"You okay?" he breathes, trying to control himself as he gives me a minute to adjust.

"Y-yeah." I wiggle my hips beneath him and catch my breath. I feel so...*full.* "Yeah, I'm okay."

"Good girl." Dropping another kiss to my lips, he slowly picks up his pace until I'm a squirming mess beneath him.

His grunts mingle with my moans and echo through the

otherwise silent room as we push each other closer to the edge. Scraping my nails against his back, I chase the euphoria and finally let go before he follows right after. With his head tucked into my neck, he groans and pulses inside of me.

And it doesn't disgust me. It doesn't make me feel dirty or used. It feels...*right*. Good. Freaking great, actually.

As we both catch our breaths, D rolls onto his back, then tugs me into his side and starts running his fingers along my damp skin.

"Shit," he mutters.

I laugh but don't reply.

"You okay, Blue?"

My smile softens before I take a second to analyze my emotions. But for once, they aren't all over the place. And it feels good to be in the present without my baggage weighing me down.

"Yeah." I rest my chin against his pec and look up at him. "Yeah, I'm okay."

His mouth twitches with pride before he presses a quick peck to my forehead. Then he lays back down. "I'll always keep you safe, Q."

"I believe you."

And I really do.

24

DIECE

"Hey, man," a deep voice murmurs as I grab a protein shake from the fridge. The door closes with a flick of my wrist a second later and gives me a view of the culprit.

"Hey, Jack." I lift my chin in greeting. "What's up?"

"I just...." He squeezes the back of his neck as his face contorts with discomfort. "I just wanted to apologize."

"For what?"

"For being an inconsiderate asshole to you and Q."

I laugh and shake my head. "You don't have anything to be sorry for, Jack. I get it."

"Don't let me off the hook," he rasps. "I was being selfish. You guys have let me stay here while the rest of the world searches for me. You've been...." He laughs. "Hell, you've been generous with your hospitality. More than I would've ever expected, and I repaid you by acting like a kid who'd gotten his toy taken away."

The guy looks like his guilt has been eating him alive ever since Will showed up and Q revealed her true identity. I'd be an ass not to put him out of his misery.

"Like I said, I get it," I reply. "And it wasn't a toy. It was your only hope of returning to a normal life after this. You didn't plan on running from the law in your lifetime like the rest of us. You were fighting for the good guys, yet still found a way to be on their shitlist."

With his hip against the counter, he rubs his hand against his face. "Yeah. It kind of sucks."

I can see him slipping back into his thoughts, replaying the last moments of his life before they were ripped away from him. I can't imagine what it must've been like to be betrayed by one of your own. When we found out that Vince, a soldier in the family, had been feeding information to one of our enemies, we eradicated the problem with a bullet to his head. Jack doesn't have that privilege.

And that's a bitch to come to terms with.

"Do you want to go back?" I ask, unable to help myself. "If you had the chance."

Sighing, he looks back at me with bloodshot eyes. "Where else would I go?"

I shrug one shoulder and take a quick swig of my drink while eyeing him casually. Once I've swallowed, I offer, "You could stay here."

You'd think I offered to send him to Mars by the way his entire face scrunches up. "I, uh...I couldn't do that."

"Why not?"

"I...I don't know."

"We're not as bad as you think, Jack." I slap him on the back. "In a way, we're set up just like the justice system, but King is the judge, jury, and President," I point out with a smirk.

"And what are you?"

"Executioner, and VP."

He laughs. "But the government doesn't dabble in illegal activities."

My amusement bounces off the walls as I fight the urge to slap my knee. "You serious? You don't think they dabble in illegal activities? Come on, Jack. You can't be that naive."

Jaw tight, he exhales long and slow before looking back at me. "I know you're right. It's just——"

"Like finding out that Santa isn't real but still wanting to believe for another holiday season or two because facing the truth before you're ready is depressing as hell? I get it. Just know that Kingston isn't a bad guy. We do what needs to be done to keep our world spinning and to keep our family safe, but we don't take any of it lightly. Understood?"

He stays quiet for a second before coming to his conclusion. "Yeah. I get it. If I've learned anything while staying here, it's that you guys aren't bad guys."

"You're not so bad yourself, Jack. Just think about it," I press. "Or don't. Just know that we've got your back."

"Thanks, D. I've got yours too." The refrigerator door swings open with a quick tug, ending our conversation as quickly as it'd started. He grabs his own protein shake from it, then closes the fridge and lifts the drink toward me in a silent salute before striding out of the kitchen.

I guess that's that.

I watch him disappear then grab my drink off the counter. With the protein shake pressed against my mouth, I nearly spit it out when Q rounds the corner into the kitchen while wearing my shirt from last night.

My. Fucking. Shirt.

It reaches just below her ass and displays her milky thighs that I had wrapped around my waist the night before. With a few buttons left open at the top, it leaves little to the imagination and makes me so hard that I'm throbbing in less than a second.

"What are you wearing?" I growl as I set my shake on the granite counter.

165

She grins and reaches around me before grabbing my drink. With a smirk, she presses it to her pouty lips and takes a sip. Her blue hair brushes against the back of her neck as she tilts her head back while a soft purple bite mark plays peek-a-boo with me on the column of her throat. The throat I was sucking on before I pushed myself inside of her. When she lowers the plastic cup, a smudge of chocolate clings to her lips, and her tongue darts out to taste it.

"Good morning," she greets me with a coy smile. It's one I didn't think she was capable of delivering. But damn, it's gorgeous. I want to bottle it up and keep it for myself. Along with the bare legs she's sporting.

My eyes narrow, and a growl escapes me. "Go upstairs and change."

"Why?"

"Because if you don't, I'll have to pick you up and fuck you on the counter."

"And that's a bad thing?" she quips, that same flirty grin on full display.

Grabbing her hips, I pull her into me before grinding myself against her. A soft whimper slips past her lips, but the gleam in her eyes is begging for more. The pressure from my grasp is bruising. But I refuse to let her go. Not when she looks at me like that.

"If we were at Matteo's still, I'd already be inside you. Unfortunately for both of us, we share this roof with more than a couple of individuals, and I doubt you'd be interested in giving them a show with their breakfast."

"Yeah, please don't do that," a deep voice interrupts. Dex swaggers into the room, then opens the fridge and grabs the orange juice while keeping his eyes glued anywhere but to her. "I mean, I know D and I are trying to strengthen the whole brother thing, but I think having front row seats to him having sex is crossing a line or two. And we already heard enough last night."

A light blush tints Q's cheeks before she buries her face into my chest and mutters, "Kill me. Kill me now."

Snatching my shake out of her hand, I laugh then finish it while Dex busies himself with breakfast.

"Any new ideas?" I ask, the idea of using Q as bait feeling just as sour as before.

He stops stirring his scrambled eggs then glances over at me. "A few."

"Tell me."

Dropping his gaze to the girl in my arms, he questions, "Now?"

I look down at her. The girl who's stronger than she thinks and braver than she knows before lifting my chin at him. "Yeah. She has a right to know."

"Okay." He takes a quick drink of his juice before diving right in. "I already spoke with Kingston this morning, but we wanted to get your input. There are a few spots that Sei used to go to regularly. I was thinking we could check them out and see what we find. What do you think?"

"Sounds like a shot in the dark, but yeah. I'm in."

"We were also thinking that Q might be able to help us out a bit."

"And how would she do that?" I return, my suspicion spiking.

"She, uh,"—he clears his throat and braces himself for the inevitable fallout—"She could walk around a few of the streets. Maybe buy a drink at one of the bars. That kind of thing."

"No. Not until we know where he is and can set up a plan to keep her safe."

"That's the problem, though. He's not gonna show his face if he doesn't have a reason to. He knows how well I know him. That I know where he likes to hang out. That I'm looking for him. But he doesn't know we have Q. He doesn't know that *she* knows where he likes to go. If he happens to see Q at one of his regular spots, then he might be more willing to visit that area again in hopes of catching her in a compromising position. He might even get desperate to see her again and make a mistake. One that could benefit us."

My arms tighten around her before I shake my head back and forth. "No. Not a chance."

"I'll do it," Q interjects.

"No––"

"I'm serious. I'll do it. I think Dex is right. Besides, you'll be there to look after me." She turns to Dex and clarifies, "He will be there to look after me, right? From a distance or something?"

"Yeah. Yeah, he'll be there. And so will Stefan and me. We'll stay back, but you'll always be in our sight. We'll even give you a wire so we can hear what you hear. We promise."

"Then I think that's our best bet, don't you?" she asks, peeking up at me. Her natural beauty, combined with the vulnerable lilt in her voice, is captivating. But it doesn't make it any easier to agree to this ludicrous idea.

Resigned, I blow out all the pent-up oxygen in my lungs while everyone stares at me with bated breath. "Yeah, Blue. I think it's our best bet."

"Then I'll go get dressed." She raises onto her tiptoes, giving me a quick peck against the cheek before skipping down the hall. The sound makes my chest ache because it's so...normal.

Even though this situation is the opposite.

Her light footsteps are replaced by a heavier set as Stefan and Kingston join us.

Rounding the corner, Kingston gives Dex a pointed look. "Did you tell him?"

"Yeah."

"And?"

"And I agreed," I interrupt, annoyed that they're talking about me like I'm not in the same room with them.

"Good."

Sensing my reservations, Dex asks, "What is it?"

I scratch my jaw and roll my shoulders. "What if it doesn't work?"

"We'll rotate between using Q and questioning a few of Sei's old allies."

My brow quirks. "And when you say questioning...?"

Kingston answers, "He means you can do whatever the hell you want to them to gain intel on Sei's whereabouts. Capisce?"

"Yeah." My mouth twitches with a smile. "I hear you loud and clear." I've never been one for torturing and interrogating the enemy, but in this case, I might have to make an exception.

"Good. Dex, have you heard anything else about the other families? How is everyone else acclimating to new management?"

"Not...terrible?" he offers with a shrug as he plates his scrambled eggs then plops down at the table.

Scoffing, Stefan pours himself a cup of coffee. "That sounds promising."

"The majority are turning to Lucca Russo for guidance since his dad was taken in during the tournament. But he's a pussy who's terrified to stand up to the Romanos, yet doesn't want to look weak by bending the knee too quickly," Dex explains.

"Then it's about time we form an alliance with Lucca, don't you think?" Kingston suggests. My gaze darts over to Stefan as soon as the suggestion rolls off Kingston's tongue.

He's frozen, but it doesn't stop my smirk from threatening to break through the surface.

About. Damn. Time.

Matteo had mentioned the idea when I last saw him, but it sounds better and better every time I hear it.

"With Lucca?" Dex scratches his jaw and considers the family. "He's...an asshole but is harmless if we can get him on our side."

Satisfied, Kingston approaches Stefan and slaps him on the back. "Then I assume congratulations will be in order."

"What?" Dex interjects, confused.

Throwing my brother a bone, I explain, "A while back, Stefan suggested a solution regarding the Russo family and offered to marry the younger sister to form an alliance."

"Emilia?" Dex's brows furrow.

"That's the one," I confirm, not bothering to hide my grin as Stefan blushes like a schoolgirl. The guy has had a thing for her since he was ordered to spy on a secret meeting between Burlone and Emilia's dad, Lorenzo Russo, a few years back. He's had a hard-on for her ever since.

"Shut the hell up, D," Stefan prickles when he catches my Cheshire cat grin.

"Why? You should be chipper with the news, don't you think? You're gonna finally get your girl."

"If Lucca says yes," Stefan grumbles. He brings the coffee to his mouth and takes a long gulp of the scorching liquid.

Kingston rolls his eyes. "He'll say yes."

"You don't know that," Stefan argues. "Your dad hated Lorenzo Russo. The families have been enemies for as long as I've been a Romano."

"Times have changed," Kingston offers. "If he doesn't agree to the marriage, then we'll wipe the family out. Lucca knows that as well as we do because you're right. We've been enemies for decades. But, unlike his father, Lucca doesn't know what the hell he's doing as a mob boss. He's desperate for someone to take over while still keeping the respect his father cultured. The Russo family is finished without the backing of the Romanos. And this looks like the perfect opportunity to present the alliance. Don't you think, Dex?"

"Yeah. I'll speak with him and see what he says."

"Good. And Stefan?" Kingston prods.

"Yeah?"

"Looks like your patience is gonna pay off. But let's plan the ceremony *after* this shitstorm has passed, okay?"

He takes another long gulp of his drink before staring at its contents as if it holds all the answers in the world. Then he sighs. "Yeah."

25

DIECE

"**T**his is a terrible idea," I mutter under my breath. With my focus glued on Blue, she sways into the little restaurant in a tank top and shorts. The combination shows off her long legs and perky tits, making my molars grind together with every step.

"You say that every time," Dex points out. "And every time, she's been fine."

"Doesn't make me feel any better. It only takes one time for all hell to break loose."

Dex pats my back, but it only feeds my annoyance. Shrugging away from him, I give him a glare that dares him to try it again.

He laughs. "Come on, D. We'll be able to see her the entire time, *and* we can hear every word through the mic." He taps his earpiece that matches mine. It relays everything happening around Blue and has a GPS attached to it in case we lose visual at any point during one of these bullshit missions.

Cursing under my breath, I ignore him and look down the barrel of the scope to check on her again.

"It'll be okay," Dex adds. He tries to get comfortable on the roof of the abandoned brick building that's opposite to the one Q just ventured in.

"And if it were Regina?" I counter, making him freeze.

His amusement disappears. "Then I'd be losing my damn mind. But I wouldn't suggest this if I didn't think it was our safest bet."

"I know," I mutter. "Doesn't make it any easier."

Lifting the scope of my rifle again, I watch Q order a drink then sit down on a barstool. She looks so timid. Like a little deer during hunting season. My jaw tightens before I tear my gaze away from her and scan the rest of the building.

"I don't see Sei," I growl.

"Neither do I. But give him a minute."

"How are you with sharpshooting?"

His mouth curves up in amusement. "I'm not Stefan."

"None of us are Stefan," I laugh before checking out the building south of us. A little black speck mars the rooftop and confirms Stefan's set up and ready to go if he's needed.

"Thanks for coming with me, though," I grudgingly remark as I squat next to him. We still haven't really...talked. Especially one-on-one. And it feels weird to dissect the elephant in the room and whether or not we should acknowledge it. That we're blood. That I'm sorry he was raised under the Allegretti name instead of where he belongs.

And even though he's a Romano now, it still doesn't change the past.

"No problem." Dex glances over at me then stares off into the distance at nothing in particular. A heavy silence that's tainted with awkwardness seeps onto the roof, but I don't know what the hell I'm supposed to say.

"Ya know...." He clears his throat. "When I was in that shed getting my pinky cut off, I thought I was gonna die."

"I wasn't so sure you were gonna make it either," I admit with a dry laugh.

He joins in for a second, then rubs the back of his neck, sobering right before my eyes. "One of my biggest regrets was not getting to know my big brother before it all went down."

I exhale, then look over at him. He looks like our dad. Like *me*.

I think it's the eyes. And maybe the nose. I can feel him studying me just as closely as I'm inspecting him before I admit, "It's messed up, huh?"

"Yeah."

"So…how do we do this?" I ask. "Do I just ask what your favorite color is and shit?"

He laughs. "No clue. What's yours?"

I steal another glance through the scope. As Q tucks her hair behind her ear, I mutter, "Blue."

"Favorite food?" Dex prods.

I picture Q licking her fingers after eating a French fry in Matteo's basement all those nights ago. "Fries. You?"

"Regina makes a mean lasagna."

"That's because Mama Romano has a kick-ass recipe," I explain with a grin.

"So I've been told. All I got from Burlone was shit leftovers."

Burlone.

My expression sours before I say something that should've been said a long time ago. "I'm, uh,"—I glance over to him—"sorry our dad turned you away at first."

He scoffs. "At first? Our dad was an asshole who abandoned his kid to be raised by a fucking human trafficker. Don't sugar coat that shit, D."

"Turning you away that day was his biggest regret—"

"Bullshit."

"I'm not kidding, Dex. He even tried to buy you back from Burlone when he realized he'd screwed up, but Burlone wouldn't do it."

The earpiece chirps with Q thanking the bartender for her order, but Dex remains paralyzed from my insight, oblivious to our interruption.

"I uh, I didn't know that," he mutters a little while later while picking at a random sticker that's plastered on the brick wall next to us.

"Figured that much. But he wanted you, Dex. I promise. It was just too late. He might've been an asshole in some ways, but he was a good dad. Especially in this line of business," I add with a dark laugh. "Good dads are hard to come by."

"Yeah. Yeah, they are."

"Speaking of which,"—I look over at him—"how's it going with Will?"

He sighs. "I have no idea. I don't really have anyone to look up to in that department, but I guess I'm figuring it out? I don't know? He's a good kid, despite his shitty dad. I think that might have something to do with Q's help, though. Will idolizes her."

Eyeing Q through the scope again, I murmur, "She's something else, isn't she?"

"Yeah. How's she doing?"

"It's a slow process, but I think she's getting better."

His voice is pained and filled with regret as he apologizes, "I'm sorry I couldn't protect her."

"It's not your fault."

"It is," he argues. The self-deprecation in his admission is staggering. "I've done a lot of messed-up shit in my past that I have to live with, and not being able to protect Q is one of them. Letting Sei get away is another."

"We'll find him."

"Yeah. We will."

Glancing in my scope again, I cock my head to the side. "Do you see that?"

"What?"

"The guy in the back corner booth with the hoodie."

Dex's eyes form tiny slits before he inspects the stranger in question through his scope. "I…I can't see well enough."

"I'm gonna head down," I announce, setting my rifle aside.

"Wait—"

"I won't go in. I just need to be closer."

His jaw tightens as he assesses me for a few beats before giving me a nod. "Okay. But don't go in unless we can confirm it's him."

"I know the rules, Dex." Then I take the stairs two at a time. My breathing is ragged when the fresh air swirls around me at the entrance of the building. Tucking my hands into my front pockets, I pull out my phone and pretend to text someone while looking out of the corner of my eye. But I can't see shit.

A dark figure approaches Q at the bar, and my adrenaline shoots through the damn roof. I press my finger to the earpiece and try to ignore the bustling street that's drowning out Q's conversation.

"Are you lost?" the deep voice challenges.

Q glances over her shoulder but doesn't whisper her safe word as she scans the unfamiliar face. "Umm…nope? Just passing through."

"Let me buy you a drink then. I can keep you company," he offers.

"I'm good. Thank you, though."

"Come on…. What's a girl like you doing in a place like this?"

Playing dumb, she returns, "What do you mean, a place like this?"

He sits down beside her without waiting for an invitation. *Conceited asshole.* My phone creaks in protest as I take my frustration out on the damn thing before it starts buzzing.

Raising it to my ear, I growl, "Yeah?"

"Don't go in there," Dex orders. "Let her handle it."

I don't bother to reply as I keep my gaze glued to the train wreck in front of me.

"Let me buy you a drink," the asshat repeats. It's not a question.

"No, thank you," Q politely refuses. Her voice is soft. Gentle. And only eggs him on.

"Come on, babe. Let me take you out to a real place. One that's better than this dive bar you stumbled into. A pretty girl like you is too pure to be in a place like this."

"I'm not really interested, but thank you," she repeats.

He leans forward, using his height to intimidate her. "It wasn't a question."

"I-I'm just here for a drink."

"And I'm here to get laid." His hand inches up her knee beneath the barstool, paralyzing her with fear as she looks down at it.

I can't see his face, but I can see hers. Wide eyes. Pale skin. Her tongue darts out between her lips to moisten them before she sucks one into her mouth and starts chewing on it until she can taste blood.

She's terrified.

And I'm done watching this shit.

I look both ways, then cross the street and rip the door to the bar open with a bit too much force. If only I gave a shit.

"Hey, baby girl. Sorry I'm late." I ignore the asshole who was bothering her and grab her neck before forcing her to kiss me. The tension and surprise in her frame melt instantly as I suck her lower lip into my mouth and taste the blood I'd been expecting. After rubbing my tongue across it, she whimpers and grabs on to my T-shirt like her life depends on it. Fuck, she tastes good.

Her fingers tangle in the thin fabric covering my chest, desperate to keep me in place as I devour her whole. And I *will* devour her.

Later.

When we don't have an audience.

Searching for the last of my restraint, I pull away and take her in. Her once pale cheeks are flushed with anticipation, and her eyes are practically glowing with lust as she stares up at me, waiting for me to lift her onto the bar and screw her right here. She's completely oblivious that the asshole who was bothering her is only a few feet away. Watching. Waiting to see if I'll leave her alone again.

Not a chance in Hell.

Jaw tightening, I turn around and face the asshole who can't take a hint. "There a problem here?"

"Possibly," he replies with a noncommittal shrug.

"Were you bothering her?"

"We were just chatting."

"Is that what you were doing? Because it looked like she didn't appreciate your presence."

"I think she appreciated it just fine. We were actually about to leave, isn't that right, babe?"

I laugh before tonguing my cheek as I flex my hands at my side.

"I think you're mistaken."

"And I think you don't know what part of town you stumbled into," the asshole counters.

My mouth twitches with a smirk. If only he knew who he was dealing with. "I think it's time we get out of here," I tell Q, offering my hand for her to take.

"She's not going anywhere."

"Trust me, buddy, you don't want to push me anymore," I warn him.

His chest puffs up like a little peacock looking for a fight. "What? Like this?" He shoves me into the bar top behind me, begging me to take this to the next level, and it'd be impolite not to oblige.

My phone is ringing in my jeans, but I ignore it and cock my arm back. Then it's game on. His head swings to the side as my fist connects with his jaw before a squeal of surprise greets my ears, and he drops to the ground like a bag of potatoes.

"D!" Queena shrieks.

Well, that was anticlimactic.

Tangling our fingers together, I toss a few bills onto the bar then tug her to the exit. "Let's get out of here."

Q

The next few days go by at a snail's pace of waiting. After Diece's freak out, they decided to stop using me as bait, and Diece definitely didn't complain about the decision, either.

Will is slowly getting more comfortable around everyone, and I've found myself venturing out of my room more often too, especially to sneak in some more training with Diece in the gym. Will's like a community kid, though I guess that makes sense. After all, they say it takes a village to raise a child, and we've been doing exactly that.

It's…nice. But it doesn't erase the heavy gray cloud from hanging over us. Every muscle in my body begs me to get some rest, but I can't sleep.

Because Diece isn't here. And even though I hate how much I rely on him, I can't sleep without him next to me. Whenever I try, the nightmares consume me, and I wake up in a cold sweat.

Nope. No, thank you. Instead, I trudged down to the theater room in Kingston's house and turned on the Hallmark Channel. It's the only other thing that can keep the memories at bay, and I'm tired of reliving them.

"Hey," Ace greets me from the doorway. Reaching for the remote, I push pause and smile at my unexpected guest.

"Hey. Sorry. Did I have the sound up too loud or something?"

"Not at all." She moseys into the small theater room and plops onto the couch next to me. "I couldn't sleep."

"Same," I admit with a frown. "Are the guys always gone this much?"

"Not usually. They have a lot on their plate. At least you didn't have to tag along this time, right?"

"I guess. Apparently, I'm not as good of bait as they might've hoped."

With her elbow on the back of the couch and her legs tucked beneath her, Ace argues, "That's not true. Diece's just too much of a worrywart to let you out of his sight, and they'd prefer not to put anyone in a body bag if they don't have to. Kingston said you've been a trooper, though."

"He's being too generous."

"Kingston is never too generous," she quips with a crooked smirk. "Well, unless you count in bed."

My face scrunches in amusement. "Ew."

"Says the girl who's been getting it on every night," she teases before having the decency to change the subject. "So, whatcha watching?"

"Hallmark Channel."

She grabs the remote from my hand and toys with the play button but doesn't press it yet. "What's the Hallmark Channel? Wait. Is that the one with all the corny shows?"

"Seriously?"

"Yes?" It comes out as more of a question than an answer.

"How do you not know what the Hallmark Channel is?"

She shrugs. "I've never owned a TV, so sue me."

"So you've never seen a Hallmark movie? Nothing?"

"Nope."

"Dude," I tell her, "You're in for a treat. They're corny, and awkward, and awesome."

Her eyes light up with mirth before she motions to the screen. "Well, when you put it that way, let's dive right in. Shall we?"

Pressing play, she settles back into the couch, and we lose ourselves in the movie. And just like I'd predicted, it's corny, and awkward, and awesome.

When it ends a little while later, I turn down the sound and ask, "So...what do ya think?"

"Definitely corny," she admits with a wry grin. "But super cute too."

"Right?"

"I gotta be honest, though. I kinda like my sexy mafia boss more than good ol' Henry in the movie."

Clutching my chest, I pretend to be wounded. "Seriously? He's so swoony, though."

She laughs. "He is pretty swoony, but now that I've had a taste of the darker anti-hero, I think I've found my preference."

Anti-hero. Mafia man. Bad guy with a heart of gold.

An image of Diece flutters through my mind and makes my chest tighten.

"I get that," I concede in a quiet voice as I catch the end credits rolling down on the screen.

"And how 'bout you?"

Chewing my lower lip, I admit, "I always wanted a Henry with a small town, a cute, fluffy dog, the whole shebang."

I can feel her stare. Watching me. Studying me. Then she points out, "Yet, here you are."

Tearing my gaze away from the show, I lift one shoulder and return her stare. "Here I am."

"Have you found your preference?"

"What do you mean?" I hedge before tucking a few strands of hair behind my ear.

"You said that Hallmark guys were your jam, but you're kinda, sorta dating a Romano now. Aren't you?"

I bite my lip. "I don't know if that's what you'd call it."

With a wave of her hand, she mutters, "Toe-may-toe, toe-mah-toe. My point is, you're currently on a path that leads you to the exact opposite of your small town and fluffy dog. What do you think about that?"

"I don't know," I hedge. "Diece's a good guy. I really care about him."

"But he isn't who you expected to end up with," she concludes.

I don't answer her right away. Because she's right. He's the exact opposite of who I expected I'd end up with. Hell, I was saving myself for the white knight with shining armor and a small mechanic shop on the edge of town. I scoff at my naivety before admitting, "Life kind of threw a curveball at me, didn't it?"

"It seems to throw curveballs at all of us."

"Touché," I concede, slumping further into the cushions. "I really care about Diece."

"I think he really cares about you too."

"You think?" I hate the butterflies that are currently assaulting my stomach at the mention of Diece and his potential feelings for me. We've never talked about it. Ever.

"I do. Diece is the sweetest of the bunch, but he's still a made man. Are you okay with his...job requirements?" she offers with a grimace.

Picking at the non-existent lint on my T-shirt, I give another shrug. "We haven't really discussed it."

"Well, what happens when they catch Sei? Regina told me that Dex has been listening for any whisperings regarding you, but there haven't been any in a long time. That's a good thing. But it also means that you'll likely be in the clear once Sei is taken out of the picture. Diece won't need to protect you anymore. You'll be able to ride off into the sunset if you want. What then?"

I gulp and pick at the cuticle on my thumb. "I-I guess I don't know."

"You should probably think about it. And you should probably really think about if you're willing to give up your dream Hallmark guy and that particular fairy-tale for a much more badass version who wears a suit, drinks whiskey, and gets his hands dirty."

My breath hitches. She's right. What if I had a choice? When Burlone took me, my options for my future were ripped away from me. Even after I was saved and brought to Kingston's estate, then taken to Matteo's, I still didn't have a choice. Well, not without catastrophic repercussions anyway. But what if I did? What if I could choose to leave? To build my life into what I'd always wanted? Would I take that opportunity? Or would I stay with D? Would he even *want* me to stay?

"Q?" Ace prods.

"I'll think about it," I promise.

"Good. Because I think he has a right to know."

"Who says he even cares?" I challenge while hating how bitchy I sound. But I can't help it. All this hypothetical chitchat is going to drive me insane.

"I'm not blind, Q." She smiles, unoffended by my outburst. "And neither are you. Diece looks at you like you hung the moon."

"I don't know about that," I hedge.

"He does, but that's beside the point. Do you want to know a secret?"

"What's that?" I peek over at her.

184

Her smile softens. "You look at him like he hung the moon too." Then she pushes herself up. "I'm going to get some rest. Thanks for letting me crash your party."

"Don't mention it. I'm going to go take a shower, then try to get some sleep too. But thank you for your insight. I really appreciate it."

"Anytime," she returns. Stopping near the exit, she faces me then adds, "And Q?"

"Yeah?"

"For what it's worth, I didn't expect to fall for a made man either, but I wouldn't change it for the world. Goodnight."

"Goodnight."

DIECE

WHAT. THE. FUCK?

knife feels like it's been plunged into my chest as I overhear Q and Ace's conversation. I'd already checked Q's room, but she wasn't there. Every muscle in my body aches from the long ass day of searching for her stalker while extracting information from a few assholes who might have information regarding Sei's whereabouts. But there's nothing. The bastard is a ghost.

And having her walk around aimlessly through shitty parts of town while watching her from a distance hasn't exactly been good for my blood pressure, either.

I just wanted to bury myself inside of Q then fall asleep with her in my arms. Instead, I got front row seats to more than I can handle.

Hearing enough of their shitty conversation, I slip out the back door and pace in the yard.

Hallmark guy? She wants a fucking Hallmark guy? I never thought I'd be jealous of a fictional character. But she doesn't get it. They aren't real. They don't exist. They can't give her what I can. What I've been *trying* to give her.

Shit!

Tangling my fingers into my hair, I tug at the roots and pull until the bite of pain spreads across my scalp.

What have I been to her? A fun way to pass the time until Kingston gives the okay for her to leave?

I just…can't deal with this shit right now.

"She doesn't need your anger," a gentle voice calls.

My hackles rise as I turn to the culprit. "You shouldn't have stuck your nose where it doesn't belong, Ace."

"You have a right to know if she's sticking around, D."

"I don't care what she does. She's just a fuck."

"Bull crap," she calls me out as calm as a damn cucumber. "You know that's not true, and so do I."

Dropping my hand to my side, I scan the distance and try to get my emotions in check. I just can't stop hearing the silence. The hesitation in her voice when Ace asked how she felt about me. If she would want to stay.

Shaking my head, I turn back to Ace. "How did you know I was out here?"

"Because I saw you eavesdropping," she answers with a knowing smile. "You're sneaky, but you're not *that* sneaky."

Sometimes I forget this girl wasn't born into our world. She accepted it so seamlessly. Why can't Q be the same?

"Why did you stay with King?"

"Because I love him." Her voice is soft and sweet. Just like her.

"He doesn't deserve it."

She calls me out. "Lie. He deserves my love just as much as you deserve Q's."

I scoff and start pacing again like a caged beast.

"Try to be patient with her. She'll get there."

"And if she doesn't?" I grit out with my gaze on the stamped concrete patio.

"She will."

My heels dig into the ground as I turn and face her again.

I'd give anything to have Kingston's knack for spotting a lie right now. "But what if she *doesn't?*" I reiterate. The pain in my chest is excruciating.

"Then, you get rid of Sei and let her go."

"And if I can't do that?"

"Then you're just as bad as Sei."

Fuck.

She's telling the truth.

28

JACK

"What is it, Jack?" Kingston demands as I lean against his office door.

"Can we talk?"

With a wave of his arm, he invites me inside.

It's still weird being here. Like I've entered an alternate universe where up is down and down is up, leaving my entire world turned on its axis. And now, I'm working with the fucking mob. But they don't seem to stab their men in the back like Reed did, so who am I to judge them?

"Spit it out, Jack. I've had a long-ass day and want to sleep."

Scratching my jaw, I sit down in one of the cushioned chairs across from Kingston's desk. "What are my options here?"

He pauses and looks up from the papers scattered along his desk. "What options are you looking for?"

"I don't know."

"Then let's look at the facts. Your superior threw you under the bus."

"Yeah."

189

"And your face is still all over the news."

"I know."

"And the one witness who can clear your name is under the Romano family's protection."

"That's the thing…."

He tilts his head and steeples his fingers in front of him. "Go on," he dares me.

"What if she isn't the only witness?"

"Are you asking permission to talk to a certain rat who tried to convince Dex to betray the Romano family?"

I clear my throat but hold his gaze. Except I can't tell what the hell he's thinking. And I have no freaking clue if I'm about to sign my death certificate as I utter, "Yeah."

"And what do you think Dominic can do for you?" he challenges. That same controlled facade is firmly in place. "He's a rat. And as of right now, he belongs to me."

"I know. But if we could just convince him to testify against Reed—"

"And how would you convince him, Jack? He's a greedy bastard who only wants money. I doubt an honest Fed has enough to sway him."

Keeping my expression indifferent, I argue, "If he stays in your custody, he's going to wind up dead. Am I right?" Kingston's mouth quirks, but he doesn't bother to confirm my theory, so I press forward. "If he testifies, he'll get to keep his life."

"Possibly. But a rat doesn't do well in prison either, and he doesn't have many friends to watch his back while he's behind bars. Even if you *can* cut him a deal with a lighter sentence, he'll still end up serving time. He could wind up dead there too."

"I think it'd be worth the risk. If he stays here, his death is guaranteed."

Again, Kingston doesn't deny it. "And what do I get out of this?"

My jaw ticks as I mutter a sentence that I never thought I'd have to. "You get a man on the inside."

"Or I could have another Romano soldier."

My eyes widen as I register his offer. Work for Kingston? Become a soldier for the Romano family? My mouth opens before closing just as quickly. Pretty sure I look like a fish out of water as I actually consider his proposition. But if I accepted, I'd still be wanted by the Feds. I'd still be hiding in the shadows. And I can't live like that.

"I'm not sure I could accept the repercussions of that decision," I answer carefully.

"It would be easier to just use Dominic's phone to convince Reed to meet him. With a bullet to the back of his head, your problems would be over."

"But they wouldn't. I'd still be labeled as a dirty Fed."

He leans back in his chair. "So, you'd be willing to be my inside man, but you're not willing to let the Romano family get rid of Reed for you? You'd rather involve Dominic and risk having your plan backfire?" His amusement is palpable, but I don't blame him.

It does seem ludicrous.

With a sigh, I explain, "If I choose to stay and become a Romano, I'd be on the run constantly. I'd always be looking over my shoulder, waiting to get arrested for shit I didn't do. But if I take the chance to clear my name, I could be free."

"Could," Kingston emphasizes. "There's no guarantee."

"No. There's not."

"But you want my permission," Kingston concludes. His chair creaks slightly as he shifts his weight to get more comfortable. Like this conversation isn't eating a hole in his gut the way it's eating at mine.

"I respect you, King. We might not always see eye-to-eye,

but I think you have a knack for seeing the bigger picture and are able to play your hand better than anyone I know. So yeah, I want your permission."

He stays quiet and inspects my proposition from all angles while never relieving the pressure of his stare.

After a few long seconds, he lifts his chin. "Fine. You can talk with Dominic and find out what your options are. But you do not move forward until we both agree on a plan. We clear?"

Pushing myself up from my seat, I tap my knuckles against the hard surface of his desk. "Yeah. Thank you."

29

Q

As I wrap my hair in a towel after drying my bare body from the shower, my skin prickles with awareness.

Someone's watching me.

Glancing over my shoulder, my heart leaps in my chest before evening out just as quickly when I recognize the culprit.

"Hey, stranger," I greet him. "Where have you been? It's late."

With his shoulder against the doorjamb and his arms crossed over his chest, Diece scans me from head to toe, so I do the same to him. He looks good in his white button-up shirt that's rolled to his elbows. A loosened black tie hangs around his neck, and a pair of dark slacks complete the ensemble. He definitely couldn't star in a Hallmark movie with a scowl like that, but it doesn't stop my mouth from watering.

"I was collecting intel," he answers me coolly. His tone screams indifference with a hint of restraint. The combination makes me pause.

With my head cocked to the side, I prod, "For?"

"For catching Sei."

"Any luck?"

His jaw tightens. "He's a slippery bastard. We can't use you as bait if we don't know where he is."

"I could try walking around the streets again like I did before," I offer.

"Obviously, that hasn't been working," he sneers. I jerk back with wide eyes before he takes a deep breath and mutters, "Sorry. It's been a long day. Dex, Stefan, and I have been scoping out a few places he's been known to go, but we haven't had any luck with those, either." With a sigh, he rubs his hand over his weary face. The bags under his eyes make my chest tighten before I sway toward him and close the distance between us. Every muscle in his body is tight, but I ignore his odd behavior and rest my head against his warm, albeit hard chest in an attempt to put him at ease.

"You're pushing yourself too hard."

"I promised to keep you safe, and I can't do that until I find Sei."

"You'll find him."

Another sigh.

"You will," I promise.

He stays motionless, making me feel like I'm hugging a freaking statue, but I refuse to let him go. "I missed you."

The seconds tick by in silence as my reservations begin whispering in the back of my mind.

He doesn't care about you. Not in a forever kind of way.

You're only here to pass the time.

He wouldn't want you to stay, anyway. Why do you think he's searching so hard for Sei?

The heat from his palm warms my bare back as it dances along my spine and makes my insecurities scatter like sand in the wind. "I missed you too."

I swallow back the tears that are lodged in my throat.

After a few more minutes of silence, his deep voice breaks it. "Did he…?"

"Did he what?" I whisper.

He pulls the towel off my head and lets it drop to the floor. As my damp hair kisses the back of my neck, he tangles his fingers into it then pulls me back into his chest like I'm his lifeline. "Did he ever talk to you about where he likes to go? What he would do if Burlone died?"

"We didn't talk much," I mutter while trying to rein in my galloping heart.

Sensing my anxiety, he starts, "You don't have to—"

"I know." I peek up at him. "But I want to help. Let me think for a second." The silence is suffocating as I search through my memories for an inkling as to where he might be hiding. Then I purse my lips. "He never really considered the possibility that Burlone would fail at anything. He was adamant that he'd take over the Allegretti family once Burlone retired and that I'd be his"—my mouth fills with acid, but I swallow it down—"*queen*. I don't really think he had a backup plan. He didn't feel like he needed one. Did you try talking to Will? He was with him…."

"Yeah, we tried. Just said he was in an old apartment. Didn't say much more and was blindfolded whenever they left the house. Hell, even if he wasn't blindfolded, he's a kid. It's not like he looks at street signs and shit."

Good point.

"I'm sorry," I whisper. "I can't think of anything else."

"Don't be sorry. We'll find him."

"I know."

The real question is…what then? What happens after Sei's off the streets? What happens to us? I wish I had the courage to ask him, but the words get lodged in my throat.

Diece rubs his hands up and down my bare arms before

leaning back to examine me closer. "It's late. You should get some sleep." Untangling himself from my grasp, he takes a step toward the exit before I can even understand what's going on.

"Wait!" I call out. "Where are you going?"

"I'm going to shower then go to bed."

"The shower is right here." I motion to the still steamy glass enclosure in the white marble bathroom.

He studies it for a few seconds, then picks up the towel at our feet and wraps it around my bare chest. "I figured I'd use a different one. I don't want to keep you up."

I can't decide if he's being thoughtful or distant, and I catch myself squeezing my hands into fists.

With the last of my self-control, I release all the pent up oxygen in my lungs. "You should stay. I won't be able to sleep without you, anyway."

"I'm sure you'll be fine," he deflects with that same icy tone as before.

"Excuse me?"

Where the hell is this coming from?

"Look, I'm tired. I don't want to argue. I just figured you might want some space, and I'm trying to give it to you."

"Why would I want space?"

A low curse escapes his lips before he roughly rubs his hand from his forehead to his chin as his exhaustion and frustration fight for dominance.

"Just...get some rest, Q." Then he heads to the exit.

Reaching for his arm, I force him to stay with me before stepping between him and his escape. His eyes widen for an instant, then return to indifference as he stares at the wall behind me, pretending like I don't even exist.

"What's going on with you?" I demand.

"Nothing."

"Bullshit. Talk to me. Something's different."

"Get some sleep, Q."

"Will you stop it?" I spit before standing on my tiptoes in hopes of grabbing his attention, but he refuses to look at me. And it kills me. "Do you not want to sleep with me anymore? Is that it?"

He scoffs. "It's called fucking."

I flinch back. "Excuse me?"

"I didn't stutter."

"Stop! Stop being like this," I plead. "Please. I'm begging you. I don't know what happened tonight, or why you're acting like this, but please don't push me away. This isn't like you. Will you...will you just look at me?"

His hardened eyes find mine. But for the first time since we met, they aren't warm and inviting. The light isn't there. He's nothing but a stranger. And it chills me to the bone.

"D...."

"I just need some space."

"Why me?" I choke out, praying he won't break my heart when I was so close to giving it to him. "I want to know why you wanted me that day in Kingston's office. Was I just a pretty face? A toy? Something to pass the time? Something to *fuck*?" My voice breaks. "Why me?"

His eyes soften and lose their flinty sheen, giving me a glimpse of the man I've been falling for. The warmth from his hand melts a bit of the iciness building between us as he lifts his hand and cups my cheek. I lean into his touch, desperate to fix this. Whatever *this* is.

His gaze drops down to my lips, but he stays quiet as the air pulses between us, leaving me with more questions than answers. We've been having sex regularly ever since I gave myself to him. And every time we connected physically and emotionally, I've healed a little more. Each and every touch erased the scars created by Sei's abuse. Each and every moment eased the ache in my chest and hinted at a future that I thought was ripped away from me.

One that's filled with happiness, and unconditional love, and safety.

But I want it with the man in front of me. The scary mafia man who saved me from Hell. The guy who watches Hallmark movies just to see me smile and taught me self-defense.

That guy.

Not the guy from two minutes ago who looked at me with contempt. Like I was chewed gum that he stepped in by accident and is left to clean up the mess.

And right now, I don't know what to think.

"You want the truth, Q?" he asks, that same tortured expression slipping into his features.

"Yes," I whisper.

"I wanted you because I knew you were stronger than you think. Sexier than you can imagine. And *just* broken enough to accept me and my connection to the Romano family."

Confused, my eyebrows pinch, and I replay his comment before asking, "What do you mean?"

"I mean that if I'd met you before you were taken, you wouldn't have given me the time of day." I can see him slipping away. I can feel it in my bones.

"That's not true—"

"Yes, it is."

"No, it's not."

"So, you're telling me that you didn't dream of finding a Hallmark guy instead of a beast attached to the mafia?"

I flinch back. "What?"

"Isn't that what you told me at Matteo's estate?"

"Well...yeah, but—"

"Don't lie to yourself, Q," he murmurs. The anger from before has transformed into a resigned sadness that breaks me. "Without your shitty past, you wouldn't have been able to see past the suits, the Romano family, and the blood on my hands. Hell, you couldn't stand the sight of me when we first met—"

"That's because I'd been raped over and over again for weeks," I cry. "I couldn't stand the sight of anyone, including myself, I might add. Where is this coming from?"

The real Diece fights his way to the surface and scrubs his hand across his face in defeat. Like the battle that's raging inside of him is taking its toll, but he doesn't know how to stop it.

"Talk to me, D," I plead. "Where is this coming from?"

"Honestly? I don't even know anymore. Look—"

The door flings open, and D shoves me behind his massive frame to protect me from the unexpected visitor.

"What is it?" Diece barks.

"We had a few motion sensors go off in the back," Lou announces, his voice laced with panic. "Someone's on the property."

"Who?"

"We don't know. Dark figure wearing a hoodie. Come on."

"I'll be right there," Diece returns before turning back to me. "Stay here."

"Where are you going?"

"I gotta go help find our little visitor."

"Do you think it could be—"

"Just stay here and don't leave this room. Lou will be in the security room down the hall. I'll be back as soon as I can."

His back muscles bunch and flex beneath his white shirt as he stalks toward the door, leaving me alone.

And scared out of my damn mind.

Racing toward the closet, I grab the first set of clothes I can get my hands on. The thin cotton material sticks to my damp skin as I pull the T-shirt over my head then stick my legs into a pair of shorts. Once decent, I run my hands through my short hair and stumble across the hallway into Will's room.

I can't leave him alone.

The door creaks as I push it open and take in his room. It's blanketed in darkness, with only the light from the window casting shadows along the walls. There's a little lump beneath the covers, and I breathe a sigh of relief before spotting the closed door that belongs to the closet. It taunts me. Daring me to open it and check for the monsters that lie in wait.

I hate closed doors. I hate them with every fiber of my being. The unknown of what's waiting on the other side. The claustrophobia that threatens to consume me. All of it. With my heart in my throat, I inch closer, then look back at the little lump on the mattress.

For Will.

I need to check for Will.

My hands tremble, and my palms are sweaty as I reach for the handle and twist.

It's empty.

I exhale and laugh to myself at how ridiculous I'm being when a hand covers my mouth and jerks me back. A squeal escapes me, only to be lost in the perpetrator's black glove.

But it's the smell that makes my knees give out. The familiar stench of acrid smoke.

His warm breath fans my cheek and makes me gag as the familiar voice that haunts my dreams chills me to the bone.

"Did you miss me, Peach?"

30

Q

Paralyzed, I squeeze my eyes shut, convinced I'm locked in another one of my nightmares. My fingers grapple with the doorjamb as he tugs me backward, treating my body like a ragdoll. I'm desperate to find some traction, but it's useless.

Elbowing him in the side, he hunches forward but keeps his hold on me and shoves me toward the bed. I land on top of Will with a thud, sandwiched between the two of them. Will's eyes snap open before Sei backhands him and seethes, "Make one sound, and I gut you right here."

Will's lower lip quivers, but he nods his understanding and doesn't make a sound.

"Good boy," Sei praises, keeping his voice quiet. "You're going to stay here and not make a peep. If you do, I'm going to kill your little friend here. Understand?"

Again, Will nods.

"Good. And Peach"—he leans forward and breathes me in —"you're going to come with me. I'm going to remove my hand, but if you make a single sound, then I'll kill the kid. Understand?"

Will's eyes widen with fear as they connect with mine before he mouths, *Please.*

My head bobs up and down like a good little soldier while vomit creeps its way up my throat.

No, no, no, no. This can't be happening. I can't do this again. But I can't let him hurt Will. He's just a kid. He deserves a life without monsters like this one. How do I get us both out of this?

Sei removes his hand and pushes himself up, then tangles his hand into my hair and wrenches me to my feet when I don't join him quickly enough.

"You cut your hair," he seethes.

I gulp but stay quiet.

"You know how much I loved your hair." Twisting his punishing grip, my hair feels like it's being ripped from my scalp, so I grimace and nod.

"Yes. Yes, I know," I cry, keeping my voice quiet.

"You'll pay for that later. Right now, we're getting out of here. And remember. You step out of line, and I kill you and the kid. My patience is gone, Peach. Trust me."

Will's terrified gaze catches mine a second time as he lays frozen on the mattress.

"It'll be okay," I whisper to him. "Just do what Sei says, and everything will be fine. You'll be safe here. I promise."

"Queena—"

"Get moving, Peach," Sei growls, cutting off Will. "Now."

He shoves me toward the balcony window, then squeezes my bicep as he searches for something hidden in the green vines that climb the exterior of the house. A long piece of rope is revealed a few seconds later.

"Ladies first."

"H-how did you get that there?"

"You think I don't know how to climb a trellis, Peach?"

"The cameras—"

"Were disabled." He finishes for me. "Your boys are looking on the opposite side of the property. Now, get moving. And before you even think about running as soon as your feet hit the ground, take a good long look at the gun tucked in my jeans." He lifts his shirt to display the black handle. "You won't make it more than five feet before I gun you down."

"Dying would be better than going anywhere with you," I spit.

"And where would that leave me? Without my sweet Peach to taste every night?" he counters with a grin. "I'd be left to find another piece of fruit, now wouldn't I? Maybe your friend Regina or Ace can help fill the position. I bet their pussies taste like raspberries, don't you?"

Nostrils flaring, I keep my mouth shut but pray to whatever gods might be listening that he'll burn up on the spot. He deserves to be tortured in Hell for all eternity, and the thought of him hurting someone else…it guts me.

His toxic smirk holds so much promise that I want to collapse into a ball and cry.

"Please," I whisper.

He ignores my plea and returns, "You're right, though."

Confused, I stutter, "A-about what?"

His hand spreads across my lower abdomen a few inches above my pubic bone before he pulls me into his chest so that my back is plastered against it. Then he runs his nose up and down the column of my throat. "I've always been a sucker for peaches."

Throwing my head to the side, I barely connect with his nose, but it doesn't crunch the way I'm praying it will. The way Diece taught me it would if I did the defensive move properly.

Shit.

I can't think clearly. I can't think at all. Not when he's touching me.

He tsks. "Seems like someone has forgotten their place. Now get down the fucking rope, or I'll carve up your little boy in there. Go!" He shoves me toward the rope, but I fall to my knees, twisting my ankle.

"Ah," I cry as I pull my knee to my chest in hopes of inspecting the damage.

Dragging me back to my feet, he pushes me again, and I wince as an excruciating pain shoots up my calf.

"Don't make me tell you again," he growls.

My arms feel like rubber as I grab the rope and rappel down the side of the house. When my feet hit the ground, I run like my life depends on it, ignoring the way my injured ankle throbs with every step. If I can just outrun him, then I might have a chance of escaping.

But it hurts. It hurts so freaking bad.

A curse rumbles through the air, followed by a quiet thump behind me.

Glancing over my shoulder, I find Sei. On the grassy landscape beneath the balcony. My heartbeat skyrockets. He'd jumped off the ledge and is limping after me, closing the distance between us one step at a time, gaining speed as his veins fill with adrenaline while mine seems to be running out.

Panting, I pump my arms back and forth and wait for the sound of a gunshot to ring through the air. But it doesn't.

Instead, I'm gifted with the sound of footsteps pounding. And they're getting closer. I feel like I'm in a dream. The one where I can't get my legs to work. Where I can't get my muscles to obey. Where I'm running in quicksand. Where my world is spinning out of control, and I can't stop it.

Then I'm hit from behind and tumble to the ground.

"Hmph," I grunt as the air whooshes out of my lungs. He climbs on top of me, caging me in with his weight.

"Please," I beg.

He backhands me with all his strength, making my ears ring and my head snaps to the side.

"I told you"—he squeezes my neck with one hand then searches in his pocket for something with his other one —"not to run." A syringe comes into view, and he pulls the yellow lid off the needle with his teeth before spitting it onto the grass.

"Please––"

Plunging it into my neck, I flinch away from him. But it's too late.

My eyelids flutter.

Then the world fades to black.

31

DIECE

G un in hand, I search the north side of the estate, scanning the premises for anything out of place.

But it looks...fine.

My phone buzzes in my pocket, and I pull it out then press it to my ear. "Yeah?"

"Get back here. We have a problem."

"What is it?"

"Q's missing."

I freeze. "Where is she?"

"We don't know—"

"Fuck!" I scream at the top of my lungs.

A voice continues echoing through my cell, but I don't hear a single word as I rush to the entrance of Kingston's house then barrel up the stairs, taking them two at a time. Q's bedroom door is cracked open, but it slams against the back wall as I shove it open with too much force. As my pulse races even faster, it doesn't stop the truth from hitting me square in the jaw.

She isn't in the bathroom. She's not hiding under the bed. Her closet is empty too.

She's gone.

Shoving aside the terrifying truth that's glaring at me, I stalk toward the security room and find everyone already there. They're surrounding the monitors while Lou plays back every second of footage that's been recorded over the past twenty-four hours.

Unfortunately, they don't tell us shit.

"Where is she?" I growl.

"We don't know," Kingston returns, though his attention stays glued to the screen.

"How do we know she's gone?"

"He took her," a quiet voice announces. Huddled in the corner of the room is the kid. Will.

Within three steps, I grab the neckline of his T-shirt and drag him to his feet before shoving him against the wall.

"Where. Is. She?"

"I don't know. He just...he took her," he cries.

"How do you know?"

The smell of piss permeates the air before Dex wrenches me back and shoves me away from the kid. "Back the hell off, Diece. He doesn't know shit."

"He knows she's gone."

"Because she snuck into his room to check on him," Dex returns. "We found a rope hanging off the balcony. We think Sei climbed the trellis then hid the rope in the vines to use for a quick escape before searching for Q. When he found her, he threatened to kill Will if she didn't go quietly."

"Fuck!" I yell again, slamming my fist against the wall.

Grabbing the neckline of my shirt, Dex shoves me against the wall. "Listen to me. You have every right to be pissed right now, but we'll find her."

"When?" I spit back at him. "How? We've been searching for weeks to find Sei but haven't turned up shit. How the hell are we going to find him before he touches her? Before he tortures her all over again?"

He shakes his head back and forth. "I don't know. But we will."

"Get the kid out of my sight. Now."

Dex's booming voice yells, "Regina!"

The pitter-patter of footsteps follows his demand before a disheveled Regina rushes into the room with a silky, black robe clinging to her skin.

"Go get Will some milk or something," Dex finishes. "And clean him up. We've got shit to do."

With a gulp, Regina pulls Will into her arms then ushers him out of the room without a single word.

"It isn't his fault," Lou mutters while continuing to search for answers on the monitors.

My fear for Q feels like it's strangling me, but I drop my chin to my chest. Q would kill me if she knew I took my frustration out on a kid. It was unacceptable. Shame fills my lower gut fighting for dominance over my anguish as I mutter, "I know."

"Go search the south side of the property. See if you can find anything. I'm going to keep looking for any footage, but he cut the power and jumbled our connection." He pauses before adding, "The bastard knew what he was doing."

I feel like spiders are crawling along my skin. Like I'm being dragged to the damn shed. Like I'm drowning. Like I have a gun pressed to my forehead, but there isn't anything I can do about it. I gotta try, though. For her.

Rocking back on my heels, I announce, "I'm gonna go see what I can find."

Kingston steps in the way and forces me to look at him. "We're gonna find her, D."

I nod, then step around him and walk down the silent hallway, lost in my thoughts.

He's right. Even if it's the last thing I do, I *will* find her.
I just don't know if it'll be too late by then.

32

ACE

"Hey," I greet Regina and Will as I enter the kitchen. His hair is still wet from a shower, but his eyes are wide with fresh fear.

He looks like a different kid than the one I'd slowly been growing accustomed to. Hell, he looks like the one that showed up on our doorstep, cradling his arm to his chest like an injured animal.

Q's missing. And the only witness we have is the scared little boy in front of me.

Regina sets a warm glass of milk in front of him before acknowledging me. "Hey."

"How are things down here?"

"About as good as can be expected." Her fear is simmering just below the surface. I can see it. I can feel it. I can almost smell it. She's just as terrified as the rest of us.

"Any luck upstairs?" G asks, trying to keep her tone even. It's funny. She might be Regina to everyone else, but she'll always be G or Gigi to me.

I shake my head. "Nope. Hey, Will, I was wondering if I could ask you a few more questions?"

"I don't know anything. I swear!" he bursts out, his lower lip quivering.

"I know," I answer carefully. "And that's okay. But sometimes we know something, and we don't even know that we know it. Crazy, huh?"

His little eyebrows pinch in the center as he stares at his glass of milk. "Then how do we find out if we do?"

"We talk about it. Even when it's hard," I tell him before inching closer to him. The chair next to him scrapes against the hardwood floor as I pull it out and sit down.

The defeat in this kid breaks my heart as he drags his finger up and down the outside of the glass like a nervous tic while staring blankly at the white milk it holds.

"I don't know what to talk about," he whispers.

"Maybe you can just tell me about how long it felt like you were driving when you were blindfolded."

"You mean when I was with him?"

"Yeah. When he brought you here from the apartment," I clarify.

"I dunno. A while?"

Well, that's useless.

I try again. "Okay…what about your room? What did it look like?"

"My room at home?"

"No. The one at Sei's place."

"Oh. It was nothing special. Just a bed and a brown thing to hold clothes."

"A brown dresser?" I ask.

"Yeah."

"Okay…were there any paintings? Anything unique about the room?"

"Not really. I found a baseball bat under the bed, but he took it out of the room."

"Keep going." Regina encourages him. "You're doing great."

With his head in his hands, he closes his eyes. "Umm…the kitchen was small. There wasn't a lot of food in the cupboards. It looked like no one had lived there for a long time. There was some broken glass next to the fridge, but Sei never cleaned it up or anything."

"What about outside? Was there a window or anything?" I press, trying to hide my disappointment. I have no freaking clue where she is. All I've learned so far is that Sei doesn't mind living in abandoned apartments and doesn't like to clean or hang up paintings.

Will shrugs. "Yeah. There was one in my room and another one in the main area where Sei would sleep."

"So, Sei would sleep in the family room?"

"Yeah," he answers.

I look at Regina. "So, it's a one-bedroom apartment."

"Sounds like it." Her eyes glimmer with hope as she stands on the opposite side of the island and leans on her elbows.

"Okay." I take a deep breath and turn back to Will. "Did you usually walk up the stairs? Or take an elevator?"

"Stairs. They smelled funny," he adds as his nose wrinkles in disgust.

I laugh. "That makes sense. Were you blindfolded in the stairwell, or would he take it off by then?"

"He'd take it off."

"Okay." Grasping at straws, I try another question. "What was outside? Do you remember anything?"

"There was a fence around the parking lot. You know, the ones made out of chains or whatever."

"A chain-link fence," Gigi answers for him. "Okay. That's good. What else?"

"I dunno? There was this homeless guy that always slept next to this dumpster."

I jerk back. "A homeless guy?"

"Yeah."

"What did he look like?"

"I dunno? Homeless? I only got close to him once, and I was blindfolded so I couldn't see. But he kept cursing at Sei, telling him to leave me alone. Sei threatened to kill him if he didn't shut up, though. He kind of talked funny. But every time I'd look out the window, he was always next to the dumpster."

My breathing is erratic as I start to piece all the information together before realizing the truth. "I think I know where Sei's been hiding."

The sound of my bare feet slapping against the hardwood floor muffles out Gigi's voice, but I don't stop and ask her to repeat herself.

There's no time for that.

"King!" I yell. "King!" The hallway feels never-ending as I race toward the security room where the guys are still gathered.

King grabs me and pulls me into his chest. "What is it?"

"I think I know where she is."

"Where?"

"My old apartment."

Confused, he tilts his head to the side. "What?"

"I think Sei's been hiding in my old apartment," I repeat. The pitch of my voice rises higher and higher as the truth practically blinds me.

"What? Why?"

"Because it's the perfect place to hide. He knows it's abandoned. He knows we would never look for him there. And he knows that it's in a shitty enough part of town that he can get away with dragging kids to and from the place without anyone batting an eye. Except for Eddie."

"Eddie?"

"The homeless guy. He always looked out for me. He was my friend. Will said there was a homeless guy outside of the apartment complex who would talk shit to Sei every time he saw him. That has to be Eddie, which means they have to be hiding there."

His expression remains indifferent, but I can see the wheels turning inside Kingston's head before he turns to Lou. "Tell Diece to get his ass back here."

"Sure thing, Boss."

Then Kingston presses a kiss to my forehead. "Good work, Wild Card."

"Are you gonna save her?"

"Yeah. We're gonna save her."

"Good."

33

Q

Stomach rolling, I peel one eyelid open while my consciousness fights to slip back into oblivion.

Where am I?

Every muscle in my body feels like it's been injected with thick, slurry concrete. My brain feels like it has a heartbeat. And my mouth tastes like ass and feels like sandpaper.

Upper lip curling in disgust, I attempt to roll onto my side and search for water, but the cold bite of metal claws at my wrist.

What the hell?

I force my eyelids to stay open and inspect the handcuff that's attached to the bed frame. My other hand is attached to the opposite side, spreading me into a T. Both keep me in place while the room continues to spin. I'm trapped. *Again.*

"Morning, Peach," a dark yet almost giddy voice greets me.

The flicker from his lighter makes his face glow as he lights up another cigarette.

My blood runs cold, then the panic sets in. Arching my back, I wrench my arm away from the metal headboard, but my only evidence of victory is a consolation prize in the form of raw skin circling my wrists. I tug at the restraints again as my desperation envelops me.

I gotta get out of here.

I can't be here again.

Please, don't make me go through this again.

"Shhh," Sei coos, enjoying his front-row seat as I struggle with my restraints. "Haven't we done this already, Peach?"

The rattling from the cuffs against the metal headboard ceases. Then what's left of my newfound courage sparks, and I finally look him in the eye. The star of my nightmares. My stalker. My abuser. My captor.

There are bags under his eyes, and his hair is longer. Stringier. He looks even more terrible and rundown than he did before.

"Welcome home." His arms are raised from his sides as he showcases the tiny, rundown apartment, then takes another puff from his cigarette. He's always sucking on those. If only the toxins would kill him quicker. He exhales, and the smoke swirls through the dimly lit room. My nose wrinkles at the familiar scent before my stomach rolls again.

No wonder I feel like I'm going to puke.

"Where are we?" I croak. My throat feels like it's been shredded by razor blades, making me wince as the words slip past my lips. I'd give anything for some water. But I know he won't give me any. Not unless I do something for him first.

That same maniacal laugh greets me as he reads me like a book. "Thirsty?"

I glare back at him but don't miss the way he doesn't answer my question. I'm not surprised.

"Come on, my sweet Peach. You love this game, remember?"

My lips pull into a thin line while I shove down the fear that overwhelms me. Because he feeds off that fear. He savors it like a fine wine and loves to watch it ferment over time until there's nothing left of the original fruit. Which is exactly what he's done with me in the past. And what he's trying to accomplish all over again.

"Baby...." His voice trails off as he inches closer to me before running his fingertips along the side of my cheek. "You know the rules. Give me what I want, then I'll give you what you want."

He's right. We've done this before, and I didn't come out the victor the first time. So how the hell am I gonna survive a second round?

"How did you find me?" I ask while silently praying he'll take the bait and let me change the subject. The blood is slowly draining from my arms, making them tingle in protest.

"You thought I wouldn't recognize you? You've been traipsing around my streets in your little shorts and your flimsy tank tops. You've been in my bars, my grocery stores. Yet you weren't sleeping in my buildings, which meant you were trying to lure me out. Isn't that right, Peach?"

His eyes dance with amusement before he sits next to me on the edge of the dingy mattress.

At least it doesn't reek of urine.

"You know, if your bear hadn't intervened at the bar, I probably wouldn't have noticed you. I was trying to lay low. But I guess luck was on my side, wasn't it?" He blows out another plume of smoke, making me cough as it taints the air around us.

"I almost took you back there," he continues. "To the basement. For old time's sake." My eyes widen with fear. "But first, I want to know if you popped that little cherry between your thighs. The one I was ordered to let you keep." His voice is calm, collected, but there's a slight flare to his nostrils and a dark glint in his eyes. The beast inside

217

of him is begging to come out and play. To use me as his toy.

"Answer me, Peach," he growls.

My panic rises, but I don't know what to say. I'm not sure I could find my voice even if I tried.

Cocking his head to the side, his gray-tinted tongue darts out between his lips before he runs it along his yellow teeth.

Then he takes a final puff of his cigarette and presses the hot, ashy end of it to my collarbone.

My entire body contorts in agony as a tortured scream claws its way up my throat. I try to wrench away from the boiling contact, but my cuffs hold me hostage, leaving me with the slight scent of burning flesh wafting through the air.

"Stop!" I beg. "Stop it!"

A satisfied smile stretches across Sei's face. "Answer me, Peach. Did he touch you the way I touch you?"

I shake my head back and forth. "No. He would *never* touch me the way you touched me."

His gaze narrows. "Shall we check? Just to be sure?" He hesitates before grinning like the cat who ate the canary. "I have a better idea. Let's play a different game." Raising his index finger into the air, he motions for me to give him a minute, then disappears from the room. My breathing is staggered as I wait for him to return, terrified about what his game might entail.

I just want to go home.

A sob wracks my body as the image of Diece comes to mind instead of the apartment I was living in before I was taken.

He's my home now. And I was stupid enough to even question it.

I just want D. I want him to hold me. To tell me he loves me. To tell me it's going to be okay. But it's not okay. I can't fight Sei. I'm not strong enough.

With a gasp, the word strong sparks my memory before Diece's deep voice accompanies it. *You're stronger than you know. Braver than you think. And just broken enough to accept me.*

He was right. I do accept him. Flaws and all. Because he accepts mine without hesitation. And maybe I can be brave for him—*strong* for him—too.

Squeezing my eyes shut, I dig through my memories of our self-defense lessons, desperate to find a solution for this messed-up situation. I need to get out of here. If I could just get out of these cuffs, I might have a chance of escaping. But how the hell do I get out of handcuffs without a key? I struggle against the punishing metal for another second before giving up when my raw skin screams in protest. I won't be able to break free. I need to convince Sei to let me loose. But why would he do that?

The idea hits me like a truck and is quickly followed by bile creeping up my raw throat.

Shit.

I'm so screwed.

34

Q

The floorboards creak in the hallway as Sei returns. A familiar knife is in his grasp, hanging at his side with the promise of more scars. More pain. More torture.

I have no idea if this is going to work or if it'll blow up in my face, but I have to at least try.

"Do you remember this, my Peach?"

I nod. "Yes."

"And did you miss it?"

I can't find the power to answer him, so I nod.

His brow quirks when he recognizes my response. "You do?"

"Maybe not the actual knife," I clarify with a breath of laughter. "But it definitely had a way of making me feel alive."

Scraping his thumb along the sharp edge, he replies, "It does. Are you ready to play?"

"I-I was thinking we could play my game instead this time?"

"And what game is that?"

"I'll need my hands to show it to you." My voice trembles with every word, but I hope he thinks it's because of excitement and not fear.

"I'm not stupid, Peach," he tsks.

"I never said you were. I actually think you're pretty clever for snatching me out of Kingston's estate without anyone catching you."

His mouth twitches with a smile, but he doesn't comment.

"You asked me what I'd be willing to do for water, and I'm willing to show you. But I need my hands."

Still, he hesitates.

"Come on, Sei," I urge him, hating the way his name tastes on my tongue. "We've played this game before, haven't we? And have I ever tried to run?"

"You tried last night," he counters. His grip tightens around the wooden handle of his knife.

"And look where that got me. With a twisted ankle, a mind-melting headache, and a mouth that feels like sandpaper. You really think I'd be stupid enough to try something like that when you have a knife in your hand?" I lift my chin toward the said object, and his gaze drops down to it. Fascinated, he tilts the blade left and right until the natural light from the window glints back at me.

Then he looks up at me. His stare feels like a physical caress as it licks at every inch of my exposed skin. And I'm definitely exposed. In nothing but my underwear and a tank top, I'm vulnerable, which is exactly how he likes me.

"Why are you shaking?" he demands.

Because I'm terrified? I want to point out sarcastically, but I bite my tongue and answer, "I think it's a side effect of the drugs you used on me. My entire body feels like a shaken-up bottle of Coke."

Licking his lips, Sei stalks closer and drags the flat side of the blade against my outer thigh, fascinated by the way my skin pebbles under its touch. But I don't shy away from it. Instead, I drop my thighs open and force my muscles to relax.

His breath hitches. Then he digs into his pocket and retrieves the key to my handcuffs.

"Alright, Peach. I'll play along. Let's see how sweet you can be."

He fumbles with the lock while I scramble to remember the techniques Diece taught me. My breathing is far from steady, but I try to hide it from my captor. When the hand-cuff unlatches, my arm falls onto the mattress. The blood starts to recirculate, sending prickling tingles from my shoulder to my fingertips before I pull my arm into my chest and flex my hand.

One down. One to go.

With his crotch inches from my face, he leans over me and toys with the second lock. Keeping my expression free from disgust, I wait to be released. The knife rests on the edge of the bed near my thigh so that he could use both his hands. But he would expect me to strike now with my newfound freedom. He's not stupid.

Which means I need to keep up this charade for a little while longer. I just don't know if I'm strong enough, brave enough, or broken enough to follow through with it.

My pulse flutters like a baby bird's wings as it struggles to fly. It's erratic and disoriented but desperate enough to keep trying. Licking my lips, I hold his stare and slowly reach down to the knife.

He watches every movement with an arrogant smirk that tells me I'm not getting away with shit before I offer it to him. "Here."

Lips flattening, he takes it with furrowed brows. "What are you doing, Peach?"

"You're not stupid, Sei. And neither am I," I return.

"And what's that supposed to mean?"

"You're not going to let me get away again. So, why should I piss you off by trying when that would just mean more pain for me?"

"So what are you suggesting?" There's a curious glint in his eye that urges me on.

With my back pressed into the mattress, I move slowly so that it doesn't startle him and reach up to cup his cheek. It's almost clammy with a light sheen of sweat clinging to it, but I hide my disgust and press forward. "I've experienced pleasure before, Sei. And if we're going to have sex, then I might as well enjoy it with you, right?"

His evil grin terrifies me as he counters, "Who says I want you to enjoy it?"

"You did. The moment you called me your Peach. I'm special to you, aren't I?"

He stays quiet, but his eyes bounce over my face, searching for my sincerity. I just hope I can convince him that it's there.

Lifting my head from the pillow, I close the distance between our mouths while holding his gaze with mine. My chest rises and falls with an unsteady rhythm, but I pray he doesn't interpret it for what it really is. Fear.

"We've never kissed," I whisper, ignoring the way my stomach churns as his acrid breath fans against my cheeks.

"No," he breathes.

"Can I kiss you?"

He tilts his head to the side but doesn't refuse, so I do the honors and run my tongue along the seam of his lips. He tastes like sour milk mixed with a dirty ashtray.

I want to vomit, but I swallow it back.

His groan is animalistic as he tangles his fingers into the back of my head and pillages my mouth with his tongue.

Sucking it into my mouth, the tears stream down my cheeks while my nightmares threaten to consume me. It's too much. Too many memories. Too many senses on high alert, threatening to drag me back to the tortured girl I was in that room.

Focus, Q.

I hook my ankle around his leg the way Diece taught me and roll Sei onto his back so that I'm straddling him. His once liquid muscles turn rigid beneath me as if he'd anticipated my move before I grind my hips against him and bend forward to kiss him again.

"Shhh," I whisper against his putrid lips. "Let me enjoy it."

Then I slip my tongue back into his mouth and fake a long moan that would make a porn star proud.

With another groan, his hands find my ass and keep me in place, pushing himself against my core.

But that means he isn't holding the knife anymore. And I'm in control on top. Just like Diece taught me. Continuing to kiss Sei, I blindly search for the forgotten blade on the mattress, but all I feel is the cotton sheets. His hand inches up my tank top, and I know I'm seconds from no return when a sharp bite of pain blossoms along my fingertips.

I found it.

Grabbing the handle, I take a deep breath then plunge the pointy end into Sei's side with all of my strength. He shoves me off him, and I crash onto the ground with a hard thump as the blood seeps a few inches above his hip bone.

"What the hell did you do?" he shouts, his face red with fury.

I scramble back like a little sand crab toward the hallway. But he's too quick. Too determined. Too filled up with rage and adrenaline to let the pain from his wound consume him for long enough to let me get away. Like a snake, his arm darts out and grabs my ankle. Then I'm dragged toward him. My screams feel like blades against my raw throat, but I don't stop yelling, praying someone can hear me and will call the cops as I kick my legs as hard as I can and claw my way across the ground to get away from him.

But it's no use. With both hands diffusing my feeble attempt to get away, he throws me onto my back and climbs on top of me. I try to throw him off me, twisting back and forth, but he pins me down with his weight and throws his legs on both sides of my waist. I can't move. Claustrophobia sets in, making me feel like I've run a freaking marathon as I try to catch my breath. My chest rises and falls way too quickly to do me any good, but I can't stop it. I feel like I can't breathe.

Then he cocks his arm back and hits me in the side of the face. My head snaps to my right while the familiar sensation explodes across my cheekbone.

Shiiit.

His fists are deadly. I try to protect my face with my forearms, but it's useless. I can still feel it all.

At least it's not a knife, I think to myself, before pushing aside the sarcastic glimpse of insanity that I'm currently swimming in.

My vision blurs with dancing black spots that I can't blink away. He hits me again. And again. And again.

"Six!" I plead, delirious. "Six. Six. Six." The safe word tumbles out of me over and over again in cadence with his fists. But I can't control myself from muttering the useless gibberish that falls on deaf ears. I know it's a waste of precious time. I know he's probably getting off on it. But there's comfort in the word. A weight of respect that should accompany it. A promise to end the pain. The suffering.

All of it.

If only Diece could hear it.

Then I'd be safe.

I'd be with him.

I'm seconds from slipping under. The damage from his punishing brutality is too much to handle. But at least I fought. At least I tried. That has to count for something. Maybe Diece would be proud of me even though I didn't get away.

I can feel my face swelling as the darkness threatens to pull me under when a loud bang breaks its way through my ringing ears. Sei's head snaps toward it before he delivers a final, brutal punch.

One that sends me into oblivion.

35

DIECE

"What's the plan?" Dex asks from the back seat as our car rolls past the stop sign. At least the intersection was empty.

I squeeze the steering wheel a little tighter and wait for Kingston's orders, but the bastard doesn't say a word.

"Boss?" Stefan prods next to Dex in the back.

Glancing to my right, Kingston stares back at me from the passenger seat.

"Depends on what Diece wants," he returns.

"You're the boss," I counter.

"Today, it looks like we're at your disposal. How do you want to handle this?"

This.

As in, how do I want to handle the motherfucker who has been holing up in Ace's apartment, scrambled our cameras, kidnapped Q, and has likely been raping her ever since?

My jaw tics before I push the gas pedal down further. The streets blur as I race toward the rundown apartment like a bat out of Hell.

"D?" Kingston prods.

"If she's still alive, then she deserves to look the bastard in the eyes when he dies. We'll take him with us to the shed."

There's a heavy silence that sucks all the oxygen from the cab of the black Cadillac before Dex clears his throat. "And if she's not?"

"Then, he's mine."

The tires screech against the black pavement as I turn into the parking lot. Shoving the car into park, we open our doors in unison then scan the area for witnesses. Other than the homeless guy near the back of the lot, it's empty.

The light near the entrance flickers like a horror movie, hinting at the climax that is guaranteed to chill my bones. I shake off the thought, then pull out my pistol and let the stairs take my weight as we creep up them.

When we reach Ace's door, I brush my index finger against my lips and strain to hear anything on the opposite side.

A loud thump reverberates through it.

My blood is pulsing in my ears as the unfamiliar rush of fear damn near chokes me. Dex lifts his chin toward the handle.

It's locked.

"Six. Six. Six," a soft voice whimpers through the door. And it's more than I can take.

The door flies open with a heavy kick, and I raise my gun in the air before surveying the apartment that once belonged to Ace. The small family room is trashed but empty, along with the barren kitchen that's littered with empty take-out containers. He's been holed up in here for a while.

Elbows locked and my finger on the trigger, I take another step into the apartment and study the dark hallway that leads to Ace's bedroom. An unconscious Q lies on the floor. She looks more like an abused ragdoll than the woman I've fallen for. And it confirms my worst fears.

I close the distance between us as fast as I can when a large shadow catches my attention from my periphery. Running on pure adrenaline and instinct, I dive for the figure at the last instant, catching us both by surprise. He scrambles for the knife at the foot of the bed, but I yank him back by his long, greasy hair before slamming his body against the floor with all my strength. Like a little bitch, he squeals when my fist connects with the left side of his face, but it only fuels my fury. His blood splatters along my arms and once-white shirt before a set of arms drags me back.

"He's out, man. He's out."

"I'm gonna kill—"

"Let Q have her shot first," Dex reminds me. "Like you said, she's earned it, remember?"

Her name snaps me back to reality, and I scramble toward her still unconscious body that's surrounded by Stefan and Kingston, who are checking for a pulse before I shove them away and take their place beside her.

"She's okay," Kingston informs me.

"Bullshit," I spit back at him. I know my anger is misplaced, but I can't help it. Ignoring my guilt for a later day, I cup her bruised cheek and cradle her head in my lap. Her nose is broken and will have to be reset. Her eyes are nearly swollen shut with dark hues of purple and blue marring her perfect skin. But her lips are slightly parted as she breathes in and out in a steady rhythm that holds an ounce of hope.

"Q," I murmur. The rage slowly seeps from my pores and is replaced with overwhelming helplessness that acts like a knife to my ribs. "Q, wake up."

A soft moan slips out of her as she nuzzles into my touch. When her brows pinch in pain, my chest follows suit.

"Let's get her out of here," Kingston suggests. "We can help her more at home."

With a lump in my throat, I nod and lift her into my arms, cradling her against me.

A satisfied Kingston turns to Dex and spits, "Make sure he's secure, then put him in the trunk."

"Sure thing, Boss."

"Oh. And find Johnson's laptop," he adds.

Then we leave. I'm just not sure if it's with my Q in my arms or the same broken girl I first met who refused to give me a chance.

Because I failed her.

I didn't keep her safe.

And it'll be my greatest regret for the rest of my life.

36

Q

"**H**ey," a low voice murmurs, tugging at my memories. I know that voice. The sound pulls me from my deep sleep like I was doused in cold water.

My eyelids flutter open. The room is painted with soft light from the open balcony window. The familiar sight is like a balm to my frazzled emotions. I'm back at Kingston's estate. I'm safe. I'm free. Which means he found me. He saved me.

"Hey," D repeats with a soft smile. But the worry lines seem permanently etched between his brows as he inspects me closer. "How are you feeling?"

A light laugh escapes me, followed by a wince as a cut on my lip splits itself open.

That same concerned expression returns full force before he runs his massive palm along my forehead, pushing my hair away from it.

My voice is rusty from lack of use, but I muster up the effort and ask, "Do I look that bad?"

"You look like you had the shit kicked out of you," he

231

returns.

I laugh again before I'm tossed back into three seconds ago as another wince captures my amusement. "I *feel* like I got the shit kicked out of me."

"What do you remember, Blue?"

"That I got the shit kicked out of me," I reply sarcastically.

"Anything else?" he prods.

I know what he's asking. I know what his greatest fears are. I know that they're aligned with mine and that he's probably been freaking out since the moment I went missing. And not just because Kingston ordered him to look after me, but because he's my knight in shining armor. Just like in the movies. Well, except his shining armor is really an Armani suit, and his white steed happens to be a black Cadillac. But still.

He cares.

Licking my lips, my face scrunches from the pain, then I release an unsteady breath and shake my head back and forth in an attempt to put his mind—and his guilt—at ease. "It didn't get that far."

His relief is palpable as he leans forward and...stops. My brows furrow. I could've sworn he was going to kiss me. But he didn't. *Why didn't he kiss me?*

Sensing my confusion, he clears his throat then presses a soft kiss to my forehead. "I'm sorry."

"What? Why?"

"Because I left you alone—"

"Sei wasn't stupid, D. He knew what he was doing, and he was determined to get his hands on me. If it wasn't last night, then it would've been tomorrow or the day after that."

"Doesn't make me feel any better, babe."

Babe.

Maybe we *are* okay, and I'm just being paranoid.

With a soft smile, I nuzzle into his hand and close my

eyes. "You found me. That's all that matters."

"Doesn't feel like enough."

"It is." I turn my head and kiss the palm of his hand. "I love you, D."

Shoulders hunched, he removes his touch. Its absence feels like a bucket of ice water has been poured on me.

"D—"

He scrubs his face roughly. "You don't have to say that just because I feel like shit that I couldn't protect you."

"What? I'm not just saying it." The soft mattress makes it difficult to push myself up when every inch of my body is aching. But I shove aside the discomfort and make sure I have D's full attention as I sit up and hold his agonized stare.

"I know you're afraid that I'm only with you because it's convenient. I know that I'm the one who planted those seeds of doubt, and if I could take it back, I would. Because there isn't any doubt for me. Not anymore."

"Q—"

"I'm serious, Diece. I'm so sorry I made you doubt my feelings. That I made you wonder whether or not I care about you. I feel something for you that I can't even put into words because *I love you* doesn't begin to do it justice. It's funny. As you led me up to Matteo's door all those nights ago, I felt like I'd been transported to the castle in *Beauty and The Beast*. I wanted to laugh at how ridiculous I felt, comparing my situation to a fairy-tale when I was terrified out of my mind. But I couldn't have been more right. And in my own way, I think I still found my prince."

"You should get some rest," he deflects. It's as if my words have burned him when I was hoping they'd ease the ache I'd inflicted before I was taken. This is all my fault.

Pushing to his feet, he heads to the door when my weary voice stops him.

"Where is he?" I don't bother to say his name. We both

know exactly who I'm referring to. "Is he alive?" I press.

With a subtle nod, he faces me again. "He's in the shed."

"You brought him back home?" The word slips past my lips before I can stop it.

Home.

Kingston's estate isn't home. In fact, I'm not even sure where Diece really lives when shit isn't hitting the fan in the Romano family. But it's home to me. Because it's where Diece is.

"Yeah," he answers me before snaking his hand behind his neck. Then he squeezes it and adds, "We figured you might want to talk to him."

"Talk?" I challenge unconvinced.

"Whatever you want," he returns with a shrug. "He's not going to walk out of that shed, though. Not after everything he put you through."

"Will you stay with me when I face him?"

His eyes connect with mine. "Yeah. I'll be here for however long you need me."

"Then why are you walking out of this room?"

"Because you should get some sleep."

"Then you should stay and hold me."

"Q," he breathes.

"Don't act like you know what I want."

"Maybe I know what you need," he counters.

"If you did, then you wouldn't be all the way across the room. You wouldn't have hesitated in kissing me. You wouldn't be pushing me away right now. I'm not stupid, Diece. I can see it. Hell, I can feel it. Right now, I need you. Why are you putting up a wall between us?"

"Q," he repeats. It's nothing but a whisper.

"Answer the question."

His face sours. "You deserve your Hallmark guy."

"I deserve a guy who loves me the way I love him. So tell

me, D. Do you love me?"

"Blue...." The anguish in his voice is staggering, but I don't let him off the hook.

"Answer the question," I push.

"Of course, I fucking love you. I love your addiction to shitty movies. I love your blue hair that's always a mess. I love the way you block people out when you don't want to hear what they have to say and the way you get up every single morning even when you'd rather hide under the covers. Because you're brave. You're beautiful. And you're all I've ever wanted."

"Let me ask you this, Diece. Do you remember when we were at Matteo's estate? When you told me that you weren't keeping me as your prisoner? That I could choose what I wanted? If I wanted to stay or not?"

"Yeah."

"Then let me make my choice. I want to stay. I want you. I love you. I choose you. I don't want a sappy Hallmark guy even if he was real. I want raw. I want *you*," I reiterate with tears in my eyes. "So, let me ask you this again. Why the hell are you all the way across the room when I just want you to hold me?"

I hold my breath and watch his thoughts flash across his face like a slideshow. But there isn't any indecision. Just vulnerability. It doesn't belong on such a sexy, confident man. But maybe that's why I love him. Why he's captured my thoughts, my body, and my heart. Because he can be vulnerable with me. The same way I've learned to open myself with him.

"Please?" I whisper.

He breaks and gives in, closing the distance between us with a few strides before wrapping his arms around me.

"I love you, Blue."

"Love you too, D."

37

Q

"You sure you're ready?" Diece asks. The shed is looming in front of us like the never-ending hallway from *The Shining*, but I somehow manage to take another step toward it. When a pebble bounces off my sneaker and skids across the cobblestone path, my gaze follows it.

I don't know if I'm strong enough to do this.

With our hands tangled together, he tugs me back a few steps. "Q?"

I blink. "What?"

"Are you sure you're ready?"

"I don't think I'll ever be ready to face him again," I mutter to myself.

"You don't have to do this."

"I know."

"We can wait until you're ready—"

"I'm ready to put him in my past," I return before glancing toward the looming shed. "Which means I need to look him in the eye one more time."

"You sure?"

"Yeah." I gulp, then turn back to him. "I'm sure."

His finger brushes beneath my chin, lifting it a few inches before his spine curves down, and he presses a soft kiss to my parted lips. "You can do this."

"I'm scared," I whisper, feeling like a small child.

"It's okay to be scared."

"You're never scared," I counter.

"Bullshit." He laughs. "I was terrified when you went missing."

Missing.

It feels like a lifetime ago, but my bumps and bruises prove otherwise.

Licking my lips, I ask, "Then what did you do?"

"I used that fear to push me forward instead of letting it paralyze me."

Being paralyzed has always been my first reaction. It was the one I clung to. But D's right. Sometimes, we have to fight our natural instincts and push past them, searching for the correct response and repeating the behavior over and over again until it becomes second nature.

Just like in the gym when we'd practice Jiu-Jitsu. When I'd want to pull away from my opponent instead of bringing him closer to get what I want. And even though I wasn't able to escape Sei without D's help, I was able to stall him until D could rescue me by bringing Sei closer. By playing his game and tricking him into letting me out of those handcuffs. Because if I hadn't, I'd have more than bruises on my face and arms. And healing from that particular form of abuse was hard enough the first time.

Sometimes, we have to pick the harder route because we know it'll pay off in the end. And if I let my fear paralyze me, I'll regret it for the rest of my life.

"Then I guess that's what I'm going to do too. Come on."

With my head held high, I push the heavy door of the

shed open. Déjà vu hits me square in the chest as I take in the bare space. In the center of the room, there's a chair with a drain conveniently placed beneath it. But instead of Burlone being strapped to it, it's Sei.

The last time I was here, I was drowning in self-loathing, hatred, bitterness, and every other dark emotion, and I was positive I'd never be able to look in the mirror without my scars glaring back at me. But I'm not drowning anymore. In fact, I feel like I can fly. Like the storm is clearing, and I can see blue skies ahead of me. I just need to finish this.

Squeezing Diece's hand a little tighter, I look at him from over my shoulder.

He's my rock. My knight. And my biggest cheerleader, although he'd kill me if he knew I looked at him that way.

My lips tilt up in amusement before I take a deep breath and face my demons head-on.

Sei's long, stringy hair hangs over his face, shielding him from view. But I can still feel his eyes on me as they peek through the greasy curtain. Shoulders hunched, and his hands cuffed to the arms of the chair, he mentions, "Took you long enough."

"Sorry," I reply, my voice dripping with sarcasm. "I was a little banged up after our encounter. Figured I could use a day or two to rest."

He lifts his chin and scans me up and down. "Looks like you could use a few more."

Rolling my eyes, I harness my fear and saunter toward the cabinet in the back of the room like I don't have a care in the world while praying he can't see the way my entire body is trembling with every step. "Thanks. You don't look too great yourself, ya know."

His face looks worse than mine, and that's saying something. Honestly, I'm not sure how he can even see me right now when his eyes are practically swollen shut with dark purple and blue bruises. His nose sits at an awkward angle too, and there's a large gap where his front tooth used to be.

At least I still have all of my teeth.

Sei scoffs. "You can thank your goon for that. Tell me, Peach, does he cut you up the way I did? Does he fuck your ass until your blood mixes with his cum? Does he—" His head snaps forward until his chin is resting on his chest. A low, mangled groan echoes through the room as Diece tucks his handgun back into the back of his slacks after he'd shut him up with it.

I hide my shudder and cease my pursuit of the damn cabinet. I just...can't do it anymore. He doesn't deserve my fear, my time, or my future.

"I'm going to make this quick, Sei," I announce before turning to face him. "You are a despicable human being. Scratch that. You're not human at all. You're nothing but a rabid dog who needs to be put down. You do *not* own me. I'd like to say that you've never owned me, but that would be a lie. You know that as well as I do." The triumphant look painted across his face makes my stomach churn, but I press on. "You *did* own me, Sei. You used me. You abused me. You broke me in ways that I couldn't comprehend. Because of you, I couldn't eat. I couldn't sleep. I couldn't even shower. You brought me to my lowest point. A point where I didn't care about living anymore. In fact, I didn't *want* to live anymore. I was angry. I was disgusted. And I was bitter. When I wasn't dreaming about what you put me through, I was dreaming about what I would do to you if you were ever at my mercy. I was dreaming about this moment, Sei. The moment when you'd be strapped to this chair, and I could do whatever I wanted to you. I could hurt you the way you'd hurt me. You'd consumed me, Sei. My thoughts. My nightmares. Everything." I tear my gaze away from him and find

Diece staring at me with pride. Those same warm eyes bring a soft smile to my lips.

"But then I met Diece," I tell him. "He managed to do something I didn't think was possible. He gave me hope. He gave me strength. He gave me courage. He returned everything you'd stripped from me and somehow managed to make me feel lovable. Beautiful. And worthy of the life I'd thought was ripped away. So, I'm not bitter anymore. And I'm not going to hurt you because you don't deserve another moment of my precious time. When I leave this room, I want you to know that you'll never cross my mind ever again. My dreams will be full of the man I love. My days will be spent in his arms. And you? You'll be erased. No one will remember you. No one will mourn you. You'll be put down like the rabid dog you are."

Then I sashay back toward the exit but stop when I've reached Diece. Rising onto my tiptoes, I press a quick kiss to his stubbled cheek. "Put him down. When you're done, come find me."

"And where will you be?"

"On our bed. Naked."

He laughs. "I love you, Blue."

"I love you too." I smile in return and give him another quick kiss before slipping through the cracked shed door.

And when I hear the gun go off a few seconds later, I don't look back. I don't need to. Because my future is too bright. And it's all because of Diece.

THE END

SNEAK PEEK

Interested in a sneak peek of Black Jack? Here's the first chapter.

Available Now

JACK

CHAPTER ONE

The lock on the outside of Dominic's door is a stark reminder of the world I've slipped into. I enter the six-digit code and hear the lock click open before shoving the door aside.

Even though the lights are on, the room is dark. There isn't any natural light from a window. It's just a box. No pictures on the walls. No drawers or nightstands. Just a camera in the ceiling. A bed. And a prisoner. Which is when I see him.

On the mattress sits a suave cockroach who's seen better days. His dark beard is scraggly, and his clothes are nothing but a white T-shirt and basketball shorts. But it looks like he's been fed and taken care of, which is more than he'd offer anyone else if the roles were reversed.

Looking bored, Dominic asks, "You done?"

"With what?"

"Staring."

I stay silent and rock back on my heels but continue my perusal of the asshole in front of me as if I have all the time in the world.

After another minute, my mouth quirks up on one side. "Now, I'm done."

Unamused, he demands, "Who are you?"

"Not sure if you're in a position to ask questions."

His lips pull into a thin line, but he doesn't argue.

Satisfied, I continue. "What do you know about Reed?"

"Who's Reed?"

"The guy on the inside you've been communicating with. The one who's looking for a girl." I keep the specifics of her identity to myself because even though I hate to admit it, Kingston was right on that count. The less Reed—and anyone else for that matter—knows about Q, the better.

"Reed, huh?" He lets the name roll off his tongue as though he's tasting it.

"Yeah. Do you know he's a Fed?"

Eyes wide, he flinches back and loses his calm demeanor. "What?"

I ignore him. "Do you know that Kingston is going to kill you?"

"Yeah, I figured that much out. How do you know he's a Fed?"

"You're surprised?" I ask.

"Only a fool would work with the Feds. You saw what happened with Burlone."

"Then you know you're screwed," I finish for him.

He gulps and tugs at the collar of his T-shirt, desperate for air. "Kingston has to know I had no idea my associate was a Fed. He *has* to."

With a shrug, I tuck my hands into the front pockets of my jeans and answer, "Unfortunately, Kingston doesn't really give a shit whether or not you knew who you were dealing with."

"But—"

I lift my hand to shut him up. "However. He's willing to make a deal if you're compliant."

"What does he want?" he grits out as his gaze bounces around the empty room in search of an escape. But he won't find one that doesn't involve helping me.

"He wants you to testify against Reed in court," I answer.

The bastard scoffs. "He wants me to snitch?"

"Yeah."

"Why?"

"Because it'll clear my name."

"And who are you?" he demands, pinning me with his stare.

"Jack." The name feels foreign. Like it belongs to someone else. Someone from a past life.

"Is that name supposed to mean something to me?"

"No. But it means something to your associate, Reed."

His dark, beady eyes narrow as he takes a moment to assess me the same way I'd assessed him when I first stepped into this room. Pushing himself up from the bed, he strides closer and asks, "Who are you, Jack? And why should I help clear your name?"

"Because Reed is trying to pin me for the mob shit he's been dealing with."

Brow arching, he clarifies, "So you're a Fed too?"

"Are you willing to help me or not?" I huff.

"Why, exactly, would I help you?"

"Because if you don't, you're gonna die. Kingston will kill you," I point out.

He scoffs. "Yeah, but if I testify, I'll be dead anyway."

"Guess that's a risk you'll have to take," I press, feigning indifference. If he doesn't agree, then I really am screwed, and I'll live the rest of my life on the run.

He shakes his head back and forth and sees right through

me. "No. No deal. I have a sister. She's the only family I've got. If I get labeled a rat, they'll kill her too."

"Kingston won't—"

"I'm not talking about the Romanos," he spits. "I'm talking about every other fucking family in the business. When you're labeled a rat, they don't just eradicate the vermin. They exterminate the whole family. If I'm dead anyway, I'd rather Kingston do it and leave my sister untouched than die and leave her to fend for herself with the label of a rat for a brother."

"Who knew you were a family man," I note, my voice thick with sarcasm. Wracking my brain, I offer, "What if I put her into the witness protection program? I'll keep her safe."

"No. It's bullshit and won't work." He rolls his eyes, daring me to suggest it twice.

"That's not true—"

"I've been in the business long enough to know how easy it is to find someone." He hesitates and scratches the scraggly beard along his lower jaw. As if a lightbulb starts glowing, a wide grin of triumph stretches across his face. "I'll do it on one condition."

My stomach twists with suspicion, but I take the bait and ask, "And what's that?"

"You marry her."

"What?" I choke out, convinced I've heard him wrong. He can't be serious. Why the hell would he want his sister to marry a Fed?

"Yeah." That same wide grin is stretched across his face. Like the idea is sounding better and better by the minute. "If you marry Bianca, then I'll promise to testify against Reed and clear your name. Like you said, I'm a dead man, anyway. But at least my sister will be safe if she's stripped from this life and marries you."

"I'm not interested in a messed-up arranged marriage—"

"Then I'm not interested in sticking my neck out for you."

"How is marrying a Fed any better than disappearing into the witness protection program?" I counter. This guy has lost his damn mind.

"Because if a Fed's wife goes missing, it'll make national news, and whoever dared to touch her will have a target painted on their back. If a random nobody is murdered, then it's just another sob story that goes unsolved, and they'll get away scot-free."

Nostrils flaring, I search for a solution that doesn't end with me marrying a damn stranger. But I can't find one.

"Take it or leave it," he adds with the same fake indifference I'd been spewing only moments before. He knows I've lost.

And so do I.

Available Now

INTERESTED IN A FREE STORY?

Interested in reading a sexy short story about Stephan and his soon-to-be wife, Emilia?
Click this link to join my newsletter and download for free:
https://BookHip.com/GXMHZF

I hope you love their story as much as I do! :)

Hired Hottie

Crush

Bartered Souls Duet

(Urban Fantasy Series)

Gambled Soul

Wager Won

Sign up for Kelsie's newsletter to receive exclusive content,
including the first two chapters of every new book two weeks
before its release date!

Dear Reader,

I want to thank you guys from the bottom of my heart for taking a chance on Bitter Queen and giving me the opportunity to share this story with you. I couldn't do this without you!

I would also be very grateful if you could take the time to leave a review. It's amazing how such a little thing like a review can be such a huge help to an author!

Thank you so much!!!

-Kelsie

ABOUT THE AUTHOR

Kelsie is a sucker for a love story with all the feels. When she's not chasing words for her next book, you will probably find her reading or, more likely, hanging out with her husband and playing with her three kiddos who love to drive her crazy.

She adores photography, baking, her two pups, and her cat, who thinks she's a dog. Now that she's actively pursuing her writing dreams, she's set her sights on someday finding the self-discipline to not binge-watch an entire series on Netflix in one sitting.

If you'd like to connect with Kelsie, follow her on Facebook, sign up for her newsletter, or join Kelsie Rae's Reader Group to stay up to date on new releases, exclusive content, give-aways, and her crazy publishing journey.

Made in United States
North Haven, CT
19 March 2023